"I'd just like to be th
But it wasn't nonne
with you," Riley added, to mak

Charlize closed her mouth, studied him for a moment, and then nodded. "Yes, of course that's okay," she said. "As you say, the baby is your child, too."

With that, she passed by him, left the kitchen, and a few seconds later he heard her feet climbing the stairs.

Whether she'd be back down, or had locked herself in her room and would remain quiet enough that he wouldn't know she was there, didn't matter. She could be invisible and completely silent and he'd still feel her. Still want her.

And still not want a marriage and family of his own.

Heading into his office, Riley hoped to God he could lose himself in work. He hoped for a lot of things.

While the only thing he knew for certain was that it was going to be one hell of a long night.

* * *

Colton 911: Grand Rapids

Where there's danger—and true love—around every corner...

* * *

If you're on Twitter, tell us what you think of Harlequin Romantic Suspense! #harlequinromsuspense

Dear Reader,

Welcome to an all-new Colton 911! We're in Grand Rapids, Michigan, right now, at Colton Investigations headquarters, and I'm just so thrilled to bring you up to speed and introduce you to a strong, compassionate family of Coltons. Riley is the big brother. He was thirteen when his first set of twin sisters was born. Yeah, you read that right, the first set. He was fifteen when the second set came along. And while he doesn't fancy himself a family man, his sisters would all tell you that he's the best big brother a girl could ever hope to have.

Especially when trouble brings danger to their door.

I love this family. And with my entire family tree hailing from Grand Rapids, I love this place, too. My mom grew up on the very street where Colton headquarters is located! So I feel well-placed to welcome you to Colton 911! We've got a stellar lineup of stories and authors coming your way...

Dana Taylor

COLTON 911: FAMILY DEFENDER

Tara Taylor Quinn

Special thanks and acknowledgment are given to Tara Taylor Quinn for her contribution to the Colton 911: Grand Rapids miniseries.

Recycling programs for this product may not exist in your area.

ISBN-13: 978-1-335-62660-8

Colton 911: Family Defender

Copyright © 2020 by Harlequin Books S.A.

This edition published by arrangement with Harlequin Books S.A.

For questions and comments about the quality of this book, please contact us at CustomerService@Harlequin.com.

Harlequin Enterprises ULC
22 Adelaide St. West, 40th Floor
Toronto, Ontario M5H 4E3, Canada
www.Harlequin.com

Printed in U.S.A.

Having written over ninety novels, **Tara Taylor Quinn** is a *USA TODAY* bestselling author with more than seven million copies sold. She is known for delivering intense, emotional fiction. Tara is a past president of Romance Writers of America and a seven-time RITA® Award finalist. She has also appeared on TV across the country, including *CBS Sunday Morning*. She supports the National Domestic Violence Hotline. If you need help, please contact 1-800-799-7233.

Visit the Author Profile page at Harlequin.com for more titles.

To my Keller and Gumser families:
I've finally found my way home!

Chapter 1

He had to get that woman out of his head. With a silent curse, Riley Colton scrolled past the photo that had distracted him for no good reason. He moved on to another, trying to focus on the investigation at hand, and instead, wondered why the previous photo had even brought an image of Charlize Kent to his brain.

The unknown female he'd been looking at via photo didn't bear the slightest resemblance to the flesh-and-blood woman with whom he'd had one night of incredible sex—and walked out on pretty much as soon as they were done. The only thing the two images—his mental one and the one he'd seen on his screen—had in common was that the women depicted were female, about the same age.

The world was filled with thirty-year-old women— all much younger than his forty-three years.

He scrolled back up one. Glanced at that picture again. Looking for a resemblance that would justify the intrusive Charlize image. There was a look about the woman on the screen—trusting, almost. *Trusting* could have been Charlize's middle name. From what he'd heard the night he'd met her, Ms. Kent was one tough cookie. A social worker in private practice, she specialized in domestic violence matters and dealt with some pretty tough situations. With him, she'd been charming, smart, sweet, passionate and completely... trusting.

The other woman, the one he was hoping to find by scrolling through internet photos matching her description, had been trusting, too. And then one day she'd just disappeared.

Charlize had left the fundraiser with him when he could have been a criminal. Was that what had happened to Shannon Martin? Had she trusted the wrong guy and met with a painful fate? The missing person cold case was still with the Grand Rapids Police Department, and filed with the FBI, as well, but his client, Shannon's younger brother, Avis, had hired Colton Investigations to try to find her. Avis had said he'd figured that Riley, with his more than twenty years as an FBI agent, might have some success where others had failed.

Since Riley and his younger siblings were all about finding justice, he'd taken the case on the spot. He had Ashanti, Colton Investigations' tech expert, and Bailey, their researcher, both working on Shannon's file, but with them out of the office on separate pursuits that afternoon, and a hunch occurring to him, there he was, alone in the office, poring over photos. He'd honed an ability to listen, study and find the truth, and trusted his instincts above all else.

Shannon, nineteen at the time of her disappearance, had choreographed an award-winning piece for a high school dance class shortly before she'd vanished. Riley knew, through carting his two sets of younger twin sisters to the dance studio years ago, that there were national competitions for choreography. It was possible that Shannon was alive, and, for some reason, could be pursuing her talent under a different name.

Ashanti would be much more capable than he was at finding such needles in the haystack of life, but he'd wanted to play out his hunch privately before turning such an onerous task over to her. No use wasting agency resources if he started looking and got a feeling he was on a dead end.

So there he was, in jeans, a T-shirt and tennis shoes, sitting at his desk in what used to be his dad's study, scratching at the scruffy growth on his face as he perused photos of dance choreographers, and getting no inspiration at all—except to be reminded of Charlize Kent. A woman he had no intention of contacting ever again.

He had no doubt that he would remain true to that intention.

But comparing choreographers to the age-progressed photo of Shannon, he wasn't feeling it...perhaps this angle was a bust...

A scurry of claws against expensively finished hardwood floors had him glancing out toward the large living room converted into the main CI office space. He lived in the family home where they'd all grown up, part of which he'd converted into the CI offices. Pal, his six-year-old German shepherd, was taking off outside, heading through the doggy door he'd had installed into the dining room wall beyond the living room. He listened for the second before she let out a bark of alarm, and, hand on the gun at his waist, headed out to see what was bothering her.

It wouldn't be birds or squirrels. She had a different sound for the wildlife prey she seemed to think were her toys.

"Pal!" he hollered, his tone filled with command. Twenty years as an agent with the FBI had gained him some dangerous enemies. Losing Pal to one of them wasn't on his list of "to-dos."

Keeping to the walls, out of direct line of windows, he heard Pal whine—in greeting. Not pain. And stepped outside as Brody Higgins, their tall unofficial foster sibling, came hurrying toward him, in skinny blue jeans, button-down shirt and brown blazer, with a duffel bag slung over his shoulder. Ignoring Pal completely, Brody glanced behind him and then his spectacled and clearly terrified brown-eyed gaze landed on Riley.

"Thank God you're home," he panted, out of breath, as though he'd been running, his brown mop of hair, which was normally gelled, wet with sweat.

Seeing Pal trot over to sniff the gate Brody had come through, and then head back up toward them, Riley, worried for the younger man, quickly pulled Brody inside.

"What's going on?" he asked. "Where's your car?" Sixteen years older than Brody, Riley had always been a watchdog and big brother figure.

"I left it a couple of blocks over," Brody said, "I

think I was being followed, and ditched my car to head out on foot between houses."

Pal came running in through the doggy door. Tail wagging.

That meant the backyard was clear of any foreign scent or bodies, Riley translated, giving the dog's head a few absentminded strokes while he assessed Brody. Though he was now an attorney, Brody had once been on Riley's father's radar for murder. A Michigan district attorney, Graham Colton had believed the kid had been in the wrong place at the wrong time, hadn't murdered the Heritage Park woman he'd been arrested for killing—in spite of the fact that Brody had been in possession of the dead woman's wallet. He had declined to prosecute the then eighteen-year-old Brody.

The kid had claimed that he'd found the wallet near her body. Graham had believed him and been proven correct two months later when DNA confirmed a meth dealer's guilt. After that, feeling for the kid, the Coltons collectively had taken the orphaned foster kid under their protective wing.

"You think you were being followed," Riley said, taking stock of the tall, skinny young man who stood there trembling. And then, saying, "Stay here," he took his gun in hand and headed outside.

His gun leading the way in front of a muscular build that served him well, Riley protected his back with walls and cover, checking out the entire perimeter of the property, finding nothing amiss. A no-gooder would have a hard time going unnoticed in that elite historic neighborhood, and an even harder time staying unnoticed with the plethora of security cameras everywhere. On his property and others', too.

"It's all clear," he announced, heading in the back door, through the kitchen, to the main office where Brody sat, hunched over, propping himself with a fore-arm across his knees as he rubbed his eyes.

The hand that lay limp by his knee caught Riley's at-tention. Two of the five fingers were splinted and taped.

"What happened to your hand?" Riley might carry some personal guilt for not doing more for the kid after Riley's parents had died so suddenly, but he'd always kept track of him and had his back.

Sitting up, Brody shoved a couple of fingers from his good hand up under his glasses, rubbing his eyes, and then, hand falling to his leg, gave a quick, hitched sigh.

"I'm in trouble, Riley," he said, his tone not whiney, but needy just the same. "Big trouble."

Thinking first of the high paying corporate law firm Brody had signed on with right out of law school, he asked, "What did you do?"

While Brody had a small string of misdemeanors on a juvenile record, left over from life with a drug-addicted mother who'd eventually overdosed, he'd walked the straight and narrow in the nine years since his escape from prosecution for the murder he didn't commit.

Riley had been front and center when Brody had graduated from college, and then law school and he'd been the first one Brody called when he'd passed the bar.

"I borrowed some money," Brody said, his gaze dropping away from Riley's. "I had a chance to get in on the ground floor of a great, can't-fail deal, with a quick return. Enough to pay off the hundred thousand I owe in school loans…"

Heart sinking, Riley dropped his butt to the corner of Bailey's desk, facing Brody, who was still slumped on a chair along the wall. Few things that promised huge returns quickly panned out. He knew that. Why didn't Brody?

Keeping the unproductive thoughts to himself, he went for the facts. *Listen, study, find the truth.*

"What deal?"

"I passed by this promotional poster, claiming you could make six figures overnight, and attended a seminar. All you had to do was become a part of this exclusive RetivaYou team…"

"RevitaYou," Riley interjected, not gently. He really needed to work on his patience. Most particularly where Brody was concerned. He expected way more out of the kid than was fair.

Especially considering the fact that when Brody had been in college and would have welcomed a place to call home, Riley hadn't taken the kid in. He'd been living alone in a place big enough for three people to comfortably stay out of each other's way. But after spending his teen and early adult years helping to raise five siblings, he'd needed space to himself. Quiet in which to breathe. He had a sometimes dangerous job that required total focus. He'd prized his solitude. He'd let Brody down.

"It's this new vitamin product," Brody said, sitting up straighter and looking Riley in the eye. "You take one vitamin a day, and you start to look ten years younger within a week…"

Riley didn't bother to hide the rise of his brow on that one. Seriously...

"I know it sounds crazy, Riley, but I swear to you, if you'd been there, you'd understand. There were people there who'd taken the vitamins and you could see the difference looking at time-stamped photos and then seeing them up on stage..."

Photos could be manipulated in a ton of ways. Even a child could do it...

"They don't even have FDA approval yet, so this was the chance to get in before big investors and pharmaceuticals took it over. The ingredients are a combination of minerals and vitamins that promote healthy cell restoration..." Brody reached into his bag and held out a little green bottle. "It's a dietary supplement," he said.

Taking the bottle, Riley looked it over. Could have been any of the various vitamin supplements he saw on shelves at the store. Thirty capsules to a bottle. "Have you been taking them?" He recognized some of the ingredients listed.

"No," Brody said, glancing away again. "I was dating this older woman... I...umm...recruited her to take them because I'd get extra bonuses, but not only did she swear they were making her look *older*, she claimed they also made her sick, and she dumped me."

Oh, good God. For such a smart man, Brody exhibited gullibility that was almost pathetic. And not all that surprising, considering that the kid had been needing a mother most of his life.

"I'm telling you, Riley, in the beginning, these guys...the scientist who invented these things was at the seminar, giving, like, a medical explanation for why the stuff works, metabolism and things that react with other things. And there were four investors who all stood up and talked about how they'd already made back double their investment. They even provided bank statements to prove it."

Riley itched to get his hands on those documents. But had to figure out how much trouble Brody had gotten himself into, first. The kid had evaded his question regarding the splint on his fingers. Had he gotten himself into some kind of fistfight?

And was the victim pressing charges?

He couldn't let Brody lose his law license over a stupid financial move.

"And it didn't occur to you that there are already products on the market that promise the very same thing? Or, that if it was such a simple thing to put vitamins and minerals together as a fountain of youth, someone would have done it long before now?" he asked.

"Later it did. When my girlfriend got sick. But at first, I was there to hear about the investment...you know...if people want to buy vitamins because it makes them feel younger, that's up to them..."

So Brody had been willing to skate on the ethics of it, to invest in selling something that offered false advertisement...on the promise of big return?

Not illegal, certainly, but...

Not the way the Coltons worked, either.

But then, Brody, who'd never known his own father, was raised by an addict and then was shuffled in and out of foster homes. The Coltons had grown up in a lovely home in an elite neighborhood with the district attorney for a father and a wonderful mother who supported him, and them, one hundred percent.

The Coltons hadn't gotten a hold of Brody until he was eighteen. Had only been able to influence a third of his life.

"Go on." He needed all the facts, and wished they were coming faster.

"All I had to do to be a part of the exclusive team was make an initial investment, and then for bonuses I could recruit new members and sell the vitamins."

"How much was the initial investment?" He hated to ask; heard the dread in his voice.

"Fifty thousand dollars."

Heart sinking, and head going on alert, Riley stood up. "You handed over fifty thousand?" he asked, not quite raising his voice, but getting really close. He couldn't even get to the part about Brody giving the money to people he didn't know. He was too busy choking over the amount.

"My girlfriend…she was…a bit older than me. Used to nice things. I wanted to get her this diamond bracelet she'd seen… I needed her to trust that I could take care of her. And…she didn't know about my school loans. I had to get rid of them before I could even think about asking someone like her to get serious with me."

Brody, who'd always been on the outside looking in where family was concerned, had been willing to do what it took to get one of his own. Riley's ire stepped down a notch or two, pushed even further back by the twinge of guilt hitting him where it counted. If he'd been more a real player in Brody's life, instead of a figure at the head of the table during all of the mandatory holiday meals the Colton siblings shared, the kid probably would have come to him for the money. Or at least for advice before investing in such a cock-amamie scheme.

And instinct was telling him they had another, more immediate problem than Brody's investment choice.

"Where did you get fifty grand?" he asked.

Looking nervous again, his brow creased, his lips thin, Brody glanced toward the back door—whether because he wanted to run again, or because he feared someone might be coming in after him, Riley wasn't sure.

"Wes Matthews, the banker from RevitaYou, suggested I call this company, Capital X…"

Riley dropped his head. Biting his tongue, almost literally. He knew of the loan shark group from his years with the FBI and had never been able to bust them—its structure was that intricate, that far underground and into the dark web.

They were a "company" that always knew where you were, but no one could find them.

And his family member was involved with them?

Straightening, Riley braced himself, placing his hands on the desk on either side of him. Filled with the calm that came when he was focused on a case. A calm that wiped out emotion. Doubt. That let his instincts guide him and show him the way to protect those he'd sworn to himself to protect.

"This Wes Matthews, where is he now? I'll need his contact information." The man had led Brody to Capital X. Which meant he could lead Riley to them, too.

Throwing up both hands, drawing Riley's gaze to those splinted fingers again, Brody said, "That's just it…he's disappeared into thin air!" The younger man's lips trembled as his voice broke.

"I'll need to see the transaction data from the check you wrote him," Riley said, feeling an urgency growing on him that he hadn't felt in a while.

"I paid him in cash." Brody was really close to full-out whining. "I called him as soon as I knew the vitamins didn't work, to report the problem with them, and to get my money back, but he didn't answer so I left a voice mail. And then I get an email from him saying he never received my money and that I had to be mistaken. Next thing I know, the phone number I had for him is no longer working and the emails come back undelivered."

"How long ago was this?" His words were short. Succinct. Brody wasn't just being a kid here. He had a real problem.

One that Riley was beginning to fear was much bigger than his pseudo little brother even realized.

Brody was scared, though. He knew he was in serious trouble.

"Three days ago the guy is in touch with me, giving me all these enticing numbers that were coming my way, excited to have me on board. Two days ago I tell him the vitamins made my girl sick, and then this morning, the day I owe my first big chunk of the payment to Capital X, the emails bounce back, the phone number is no longer in service and the RevitaYou website is down, too."

Quelle surprise.

Brody had done what he could, though. He'd tried.

"And it turns out that if you don't pay back the money you owe to Capital X *when* you owe it, includ-

ing interest, two goons will show up at your place of
business, request a meeting, and then break two of your
bones, with a promise to break two more each time you
miss a payment." Brody held up his newly taped ring
and pinky fingers. "This was the handshake that happened in the lobby of the professional building where I
work." Brody worked as a very junior corporate attorney, and Riley had gotten the implication that Brody's
position was tenable. He wouldn't have it for long if
thugs continued to show up.

Riley's gut clenched. He consciously relaxed it.
Brody needed him focused. "How sure are you that
they were following you here?"

"Honestly?" Brody shook his head, his cheeks
drooped and his gaze beaten. "I have no idea. I'm pretty
sure they were, but I can't really say if it was real or
just fear that had me thinking so. As soon as they left,
I got in my car, stopped at a drugstore clinic, had my
fingers taped and came here."

Brody pulled some brochures out of his bag, handed
them to Riley. "I got these at the seminar I attended,"
he said. "I was a class 'A' idiot. I get that, but I need
the family's help, Riley. Professionally. Please. You
have to find Matthews. Get my money back. Capital
X is charging me thirty percent interest on top of the
fifty grand. There's no way I can pay all that back…"

Riley sure as hell didn't have a quick sixty-five thousand dollars sitting around in liquid cash. And was
fairly certain none of his siblings did, either. What he
did have was a family team of part-time investigators,
full-time lawyers, a crime-scene investigator, too, all
with their own accesses to databases and contacts.

"Stay right here," he said to Brody. "As in, don't

move from that seat. I'm going to make some phone calls to the others and see what we can find out."

Riley moved swiftly to his office, had his phone at his ear and already ringing through by the time he made it to his desk. And while he talked to his sister, Sadie, a twenty-eight-year-old crime-scene investigator, he was scrolling through a password-secured list of his own contacts from the underbelly of the criminal world. Sadie, who had a particular soft spot for Brody, told Riley she was going to see what she could find out about either Wes Matthews or Capital X. She planned also to call her twin sister, Victoria, a JAG attorney. They both had a lot of law enforcement connections.

He called Kiely next. At thirty years old, the full-time professional investigator sister worked freelance for the FBI and various police departments. Kiely assured him that she'd see what she could find out. She also asked Riley to tell Brody to be careful and said she'd call her twin sister, Pippa, also an attorney.

When he was satisfied that he had all four of his biological siblings on board, he phoned Griffin, their officially adopted brother. He didn't call Griffin last because the thirty-two-year-old was any less a family member, but because, as an adoption attorney, he had fewer skills to help solve the immediate problem— keeping Brody safe. Griffin also asked some questions he wasn't yet prepared to answer—he had some hesitation about getting Colton Investigations involved with something as big as Capital X. But he agreed to attend a meeting that evening with the rest of the siblings to discuss the situation.

As satisfied with his progress as he was going to be, Riley sent off a quick email to a former confidential informant with ties to white-collar crime, asking for a meeting as soon as possible.

And, fewer than ten minutes after vacating the main office, he was heading back to Brody.

Pal was there, sitting by the archway through to the dining room and kitchen.

There was no sign of Brody. Or his bag.

Chapter 2

Worried, Riley spent the next hour looking for Brody. After searching the house and then looking at the security camera footage and seeing the younger man leaving out the front door, he drove to Brody's place first, and then through the neighborhoods between Heritage Hill, where Brody had shown up on foot at the CI offices, and the fancy corporate office building where Brody worked. He canvassed on foot, too, the area where Brody had said he'd left his car, areas around his home. He saw no sign of either Brody or his vehicle, and assumed that the younger man had at least made it back to his mode of transportation.

Hoped he'd gotten safely away. Didn't make sense that Brody would come to him for help and then just run off for no reason.

He'd texted and called with no response. And then,

when he was getting ready to call the police, Brody finally picked up. Thank God.

Telling Riley that Pal had been out back and acting like someone was coming, Brody said he'd snuck quietly out the front door and made his way back to his car. He was currently driving around with his phone off so he couldn't be pinged or traced. Brody's street skills eased Riley's worry a small bit. But not enough.

"Listen, I understand you're scared, man, but we've got this," Riley told him, hoping he wasn't going to let the kid down. He'd been thirteen when his parents had given him siblings—two at once. By that time, he'd been ready to spread his own wings. And by the time Brody had come around, another set of twins and an adopted sibling later, Riley had been pretty much out of any more space under his massive wings. Maybe if he'd...

"I've talked to everyone and we're having a meeting tonight at the office," Riley continued, instilling confidence, reassurance into his tone. Hoping he was obliterating the frustration he felt. He'd woken that morning with two cases awaiting him, and a list of to-dos that had already been an overreaching challenge. "I've made a call to someone who owes me a favor and I'm working on a safe house for you, too," he added. "Where are you now?"

"I don't know. In the middle of nowhere. I drove north."

"You need to come back, man," Riley told him. "Get to my house and we'll take care of you from there."

"Okay."

"I'm serious, Brody. We need access to you if we're going to be able to help you. You're the only witness we've got."

"I know."

"We'll keep you someplace safe, and we're going to solve this."

"I don't know how to thank you, Riley." The younger man sounded as though he was about to break at any moment.

"Just get your ass home and let me concentrate on figuring this out," Riley told him, heading back to CI headquarters himself.

"I'm going to stop for something to eat and then I'll be there," Brody told him. "I haven't had anything since last night…"

Because he'd been too sick to eat? About to tell Brody that there was food at the house, Riley changed his mind. Let the man have some small sense of control.

"Fine. Just get there." His siblings weren't arriving until eight or so, after everyone was done with their full-time jobs.

"And, Brody?"

"Yeah?"

"Watch your back."

"I can promise you, I'm doing that." Brody sounded almost as though he'd made up his mind to do whatever it took, and Riley, reminded that the kid had spent some years on the street before he'd come to Graham Colton's attention, hoped that Brody knew enough to trust him and his siblings to save him, just as their father had done.

Brody didn't show up over the next hour. Or the one after that. Riley texted him. Multiple times. All with no response.

With his siblings doing what they could, and waiting to hear from his own CI, he'd put aside work on the cold missing persons case, to tend to the second case on his plate: a woman whose soon-to-be ex-husband, a judge, was abusing his power to strip her of everything she had, including their children. He'd been claiming she'd done things she hadn't done and Riley and the CI team had been hired by the wife to find evidence that she hadn't done them, that he was abusing power, or both.

The problem wasn't so much finding someone who could corroborate the wife's story as it was finding anyone, attorneys included, who'd go against the judge husband. They had to appear in his court on other cases. And that family's accountant, who had pertinent information about the finances she'd supposedly misused, still handled the judge's personal money and had filed a medical excuse from work for the immediate future.

Riley texted Brody again. Still no response. *Damn.*

Brody had said he was keeping his phone off. Riley could only hope that he'd show up at CI that night. Or at least turn his phone on long enough to let them know where he was.

That he was okay.

If he wasn't okay, if Matthews or Capital X had really been after him, if they'd intended to do more than break two of his fingers that morning, if they'd caught up with him…

Then Riley and his siblings had to find out who "they" were sooner than possible.

With Ashanti at her desk in the main office, and Bailey out visiting people on the list the judge's wife had given them, Brody sat behind his closed door and picked up the brochures Brody had left, looking for any clue that could lead them somewhere.

Ashanti was already calling all the printers in town. If they could find where the pamphlets were printed, they could possibly find out who'd had them done. If she got supremely lucky, and she often did, she might even be able to get an address of that person.

Riley was looking for something, anything, a little less untraceable. Something in verbiage that could tell him anything about Wes Matthews or the people behind RevitaYou. Was it just Matthews? Or was he merely working for someone else? Someone with a lot more money and power, someone who could afford to hire a scientist to create a possibly harmful product?

As he opened one of the tri-fold RevitaYou consumer sales brochures, a card fell out. While it was the size of a business card, it was aged, brocade, printed with a raised font, as though from a printing machine rather than a digital printer.

And bore simply a name, address and phone number. An old-fashioned calling card.

Blythe Kent.

It couldn't be.

His first thought repeated itself, a number of times, as he stared at that card.

Could there be more than one Blythe Kent who, lived on the same street as Charlize Kent, who'd said, when he'd told her where he worked, that she lived on a road he knew, just a few streets away. She'd also said she lived with her elderly aunt. It was one of the reasons they'd gotten a room at the hotel where the fundraiser had been. Because she lived with her aunt.

And because they'd both had some to drink.

And…chances were good they wouldn't have made it home with all their clothes in place if they'd had to sit in the back of a cab to get to her street. Or to his.

He hadn't offered his place up as a possibility.

He never did that. Not ever.

In retrospect it probably would have been better if he'd given the All Welcome fundraiser a miss altogether. But he wanted the community center Charlize was trying to get built in an underprivileged area of their great city…

Why did Brody have Blythe Kent's calling card? And why was it mixed in with the RevitaYou brochures?

The obvious answer was that Blythe was somehow involved with the product. Question was, *how* involved? Was she working with Wes Matthews?

The idea, though abhorrent as it was, considering that her niece was the woman who'd given him the most incredible sex of his life, also held merit. An older woman would be a perfect front if one was trying to deceive people, to make them feel as though they could trust you.

It was also possible that Blythe had been at the seminar with Brody and had offered the young man her card simply because she was old-fashioned and liked him.

People tended to gravitate to the young man now that he'd cleaned up his life. Brody was…accessible. Likeable.

Not at all the unemotional, standoffish version of a man Riley knew he had become over the years.

Grabbing his cell phone off his desk, he texted Brody again. And then pressed Call. Still no response.

But he did see a reply from his old informant, telling him he had nothing to give him.

Riley slid Blythe Kent's calling card into his pocket. After he checked his gun by habit, he grabbed his keys and, stopping only to let Ashanti know that he'd be out for a bit, headed out for the few blocks walk to the town house his memorable one-night stand shared with her elderly aunt.

At the moment, that old woman was the only one who could provide any of the answers he sought.

And in order to get them he was going to have to face a woman who had good reason to dislike him.

Charlize Kent didn't usually walk to the store or much of anywhere. She exercised on a treadmill at home when necessary, or on the track at the gym, but when she had a place to be, she just wanted to get there.

Except, of course, when she was on a mission to find answers she didn't want. In that case, she'd decided that the procrastination the walk provided was only second to its physical benefit in the warmth of an overcast summer afternoon. She'd made it to the drugstore in less than ten minutes. Had slowed her sandaled footsteps during the trek home, the small, thin white plastic bag dangling from her fingers brushing against the flowing skirt of her sleeveless blue dress, weighing her down.

The box inside wasn't heavy but the news its contents was about to bring her could change her entire life forever.

In all of the ways she'd imagined her life, her future, she'd never, ever seen herself as someone who'd end up with life changing results from a one-night stand. Until three months before, she'd never even considered the possibility of participating in one. Would never ever have knowingly gone into one.

She was the woman who, at thirty, with a masters in clinical social work, had still believed she'd find her one true love.

Had being the operative word. Now she was just a woman who'd fallen for a gorgeous face with a slightly scraggly beard, who'd let her naive beliefs lead her into being a fool and who now had to face the consequences.

On her own, thank you very much.

Her choice.

Her *insistence*, more like.

She might not have a clear plan that took her past the next half hour, but she knew one thing for certain: Riley Colton would never know what she'd thought their night together had meant. And he was never, ever going to know about, or meet, anyone who might have resulted from that night.

If there was a baby—and the *if* was getting smaller and smaller with every week that passed without a period, with every footstep she took toward home and the bathroom—that baby would be a Kent, period. Any Colton contribution would forever remain biological only.

The man had acted like she was peanut butter to his jelly, like he'd been as fascinated by her, as inexplicably drawn to her, as she'd been to him. And then, as soon as he'd had his pleasures for the third and obviously last time, he'd gotten up from the luxurious sheets they'd rented together, put on his clothes and without as much as an "I'll call you," or even a "I had a great time," had walked out on her. Never to be heard from again.

A man who'd behave so abominably, who'd turn his back with such lack of compassion, would be at risk of doing the same to any child he'd created.

Good riddance to him was all she could say.

And hoped to hell that someday the memory of him—how his abrupt departure and its finality had cast such doubt inside her, replacing her belief in one true love—would fade into the same oblivion that had sucked him up.

If she was going to have lifelong, lasting repercussions from that night, she was going to do so with joy and love in her heart. Which was why she had to get the man out of her psyche. The feelings that thoughts of him instilled inside her were not good.

As she neared the town house she shared with her elderly aunt, anxiety returned in full force. She fought it back. Running through a list of her strengths. Financially, she'd be fine. Emotionally, who was better equipped to run a family than one who spent her days teaching other families healthy ways to live together? And… What was that vehicle doing?

A small black pickup seemed to be headed straight toward her! Jumping the curb, it came up on the sidewalk and was pointed right at her. She started to run and the pickup veered, missing her only by a foot or two as a male voice rang out, screaming, "*Mind your own business or I'll end you!*"

The truck swerved back on the road at the last second, speeding away before she could form a coherent thought, the message from its driver ringing so loudly in her mind she couldn't hear anything else.

Still in shock, she heard footsteps racing toward her and screamed, dropping her bag as she ran behind some hedges in front of their building. Panting. Shaking all over.

Vaguely aware that she'd just trapped herself with nowhere to run, she heard the steps slow as they got closer and she caught a glimpse of her pursuer's face.

Oh, God. It couldn't be.

Fate had a cruel sense of humor.

Her psyche was superimposing…

With a face clearly filled with concern, a tall, dark man with a scruffy beard glanced from her to the now-empty street.

"Are you okay?"

Nope, no mind tricks going on… She knew that voice. It had seduced her…

What kind of sick irony brought Riley Colton to her rescue?

"I'm fine," she told him, still shaking, and maybe not just from the threat that had been so violently delivered. She wasn't fine. She wanted to throw herself in the ex–FBI agent's arms and find protection there… for the brief second it took her to take a breath and take back the sense of control the near miss with the truck had stolen from her. Then she'd be well enough to convincingly pretend she was fine.

He was looking her over as though he'd be able to detect signs of broken bones through her skin when, in fact, she hadn't been touched. She shivered again. Pretended it was a leftover residual of fear.

"I saw what happened," he said. "There was no license plate, but I got the make and model of the truck. Did you recognize the driver?"

Shaking her head, she said, "I think he was male, but I was too shocked by the truck itself, watching that bumper…"

She tried to relive the incident, knowing she had to help herself, to figure out who'd just threatened her.

"He told me to mind my own business or he'd end me." The exact words continued their internal replay.

"Did you recognize the voice?"

You'd think she would have if it was someone she knew, but…she shook her head.

"Your job, you talked about your caseload—specializing in potential and reported domestic violence situations—those are some of the most dangerous cold calls for cops to take and as a social worker, you do home visits…"

The intense tone in his voice was doing nothing to help her calm down. He was acting like she'd been shot—or had actually been hurt. He was scaring her. Making her feel helpless again. And she couldn't have that. Why was he even there?

"I'm a big girl, Mr. Colton." She continued, "I can handle the kind of stuff my job hands out to me—it's men who walk out on me at two in the morning who cause real damage."

She regretted the words before they were even fully out of her mouth. Couldn't believe she'd actually said them aloud. Oh God, she'd known, with two missed periods going on a third, that she had to be pregnant. Only hormones could make her say something like that.

"How many home visits did you do today?" Riley asked, his gaze more pierced, but right on track. Why should she be surprised? The man had shown the same lack of emotion when he'd left her, the one and only night they'd spent with each other.

Two could play his game. "I've done five in the past two days, all here in Grand Rapids, two of which required a police escort for my safety. Any one of those abusers, and others, as well, could be behind this. If someone had a court date today and lost, or has an upcoming court date…"

They could stand there all day, talking. With the immediate danger gone, she needed to collect her bag from the grass where she'd dropped it down by the sidewalk, get inside, call the police to make a report and continue on with her life.

Without Riley Colton anywhere around, thank you very much.

After pulling out his phone, Riley pressed speed dial for Michaela Martin, the front desk cop at the Grand Rapids Metropolitan Police Department. He stood directly in front of Charlize, keeping his body between her and the street, with only the building behind her, as he gave a full description of what he'd seen. Thank God he'd arrived when he had. And when Michaela asked to speak with Charlize, he handed his phone over to her.

Her report was as professional as his had been. She was one hell of a conundrum. A beautiful lady, standing there all perfect and delicious-looking with those fine-boned features that camouflaged a strength that drew him. With that long dark hair, those so darkly expressive eyes that hid as much as they revealed…

The woman had just had her life threatened and there he was, ogling over her. When he had a missing sibling and her aunt as the only viable lead at the moment.

"I intended to do that myself," Charlize said, handing him back his phone after she concluded the call and started to step past him.

Riley moved before she could get by him, keeping himself between her and the street as they made their way down the slight hill in the yard to the sidewalk. Other than the one speeding truck, the neighborhood was quiet—not a single person out on the block other than them. No other obvious threats. He was the first to reach the bag she'd dropped, bent to pick it up.

"It's fine, I can get it," she said and grabbed for the bag. "I...thank you for...well, thank you. This is me." She pointed to the steps leading up to a small landing and front door, and turned as though she was going to leave him standing there.

Except that he didn't let go of the bag. Instead, he stood there staring, holding on to the thin, white, translucent plastic as though if he didn't let go, there would be no progression from the product he'd seen in that bag to what he didn't want to find out. She had a pregnancy test.

And he was struggling to drag air through his lungs.

"I'll take that," she said again, pulling at the bag with a bit more force.

He had to talk to her aunt. He was *there* to talk to her aunt—not her, despite their night together. If he focused on that the panic dissipated. He just had to ask if her aunt was home. Looking up to do so, he met that brown stormy gaze and asked, "Is this about that night?"

Eloquence had never been his strong suit.

"Yes, of course it's about that night," she said, grabbing the bag. "Contrary to what you obviously thought, I'm not the type of woman who has one-night stands. That was my one. And my only."

He nodded. Did some quick math. Three months… more than one missed cycle…chances were not good the test would be negative.

Damn.

He wanted to tell her he wasn't a one-night stand type of guy, either, but wasn't going to lie to her on top of everything else. He didn't have them often, but they were the only kind of nights he shared with women.

Which mattered not at all to the problem at hand. Panicking wasn't going to help, either.

He was a man severely on the verge of that.

"You planning to take this now?"

If she wasn't, he was going to do what he could to convince her to do so. Facts were most definitely needed. Immediately.

Before he said something inane like admitting that there was no way he could be a father. That he wasn't dad material.

That his life had too much danger in it to be safe for a child.

That he'd raised all the kids he had the wherewithal to raise.

That he was too old…

Her head bobbed slightly to the left, then the right. Not a nod, or a shake.

"I'll wait," he told her.

And sat down on the step to do just that.

Chapter 3

He couldn't stay. She couldn't have him there. Not at her house. In her space. And with her mind clearing as she went into self-protection mode, something else occurred to her.

"Why were you here?" she asked the man sitting on her front steps as though he planned to stay as long as it took.

She could call the police. Have him removed. No matter how tall and strong he was. If he thought he was going to come waltzing back into her life for another quickie, he had some learning to do. He'd had all of Charlize Kent he was ever going to get.

"That can wait." He stood, his expression not quite as penetrating as he glanced at her. "Until after we get the test results."

She wanted to argue. To insist he tell her why he'd

been walking down her street toward her house. But sensed that he wasn't going to give up on this one. And perhaps the reason no longer mattered.

Or maybe it did. Maybe he'd been on his way to see her. To explain. Apologize.

Glancing at his gorgeous face, the scruffy beard seeming to hide what she needed to see, to hide all expression, she reprimanded herself.

Really? Even now she was going to try to see fairy tales where there were none?

Angry again, she stood there, bag in hand. Contemplated options while he stood silently, toe to toe with her, saying nothing.

Oh, she could have him removed from her property, but the sidewalk was a public thoroughfare. In front of her house. Down from her house. Across the street from her house.

And she could get him for stalking if he hung out for any length of time in any of those places.

But the bottom line was, he had a right to the test result. Now that he knew there was need of a test. The responsibility for the act that had created their current situation was as much on him as it was on her. And she had to hand it to him; he was being decent about it. For the moment at least. He wasn't losing his cool, wasn't laying blame.

With a nod of her head, and a knot in her stomach, she led him up the stairs, unlocked the front door and felt his warmth at her back as he followed her inside.

He'd talk with the aunt while Charlize did what she had to do. It would speed up his retreat out of there when the test was through. His brain focused, popped up decisions in quick succession as was normal when his adrenaline was pumping.

One fact was very clear. Marriage and parenthood were not on the table. And forty-three years of going without it was good precedent.

"Is your aunt here?" he asked, looking around the immaculate, well-sized living room she led him into off from the front foyer. She'd told him she lived with an aunt. The question was understandable.

"She is, but don't worry, she won't be out. She's got a migraine today. She took a headache pill about an hour ago and went in to lie down."

One plan felled. He'd text Brody while Charlize was taking the test. Maybe he'd get lucky and the young attorney would answer. He could also check with someone at CI headquarters to see if perchance he'd shown up at the house with his cell phone still off. That would be the best-case scenario…

"Does she know about…this situation?" he heard himself ask when his brain had clearly been told to focus on finding Brody's answers.

"No. No one does," she said. Which told him that she'd spent the past two months at least, probably more like two and a half, carrying the situation around on her own. Worrying. Which made him feel like crap.

Made him want to know what kind of thoughts had been running through her head all those weeks—other than an obvious dislike of him, that was. Did she want to be a mother someday? To get married and raise a family of kids? It wasn't something they'd talked about.

Just like he hadn't bothered to mention that he was just a one up kind of guy. He always let the women he was with know what not to expect from him. Having any more family to look after didn't appeal to him. At all. Hadn't since he'd left home. And with so many years of work that touched the darkest side of life, he felt like more of a risk to any potential wife or kid than ever. Why hadn't he been clear with her?

Not coming up with any answer he liked to that question, he sat there, a low life cringing with shame.

"I'll…be back," she said, leaving him standing there at the archway into the living room as she disappeared out another archway and off into the house.

Standing there in his jeans and tennis shoes, he didn't feel like sitting down. Didn't feel welcome. Not that he blamed her. He wouldn't want him around, either, after the way he'd hoofed it out on her.

He walked around, looking at the bookshelves, wondering if it was Charlize or her aunt who liked to read historical novels. Didn't care enough about reading material to follow through with any suppositions. Zipped straight to telling himself she wasn't pregnant instead.

He was not about to find out he was going to be a father.

This was just a blip in a day that turned out to be filled with them. A distracting sidebar that would turn out to be nothing.

As the tightening of his muscles became uncomfortable enough for him to notice, he stood at the window and focused on the scene he'd witnessed just moments before when the truck had almost run over Charlize. He was waiting to hear back from Michaela. Either someone would need to come to Charlize's house for a statement, or they'd need to go down to the station. Which they could do separately.

Better yet, a CSI like Sadie could come talk to her,

to take photos of the tire tracks on the sidewalk and in the grass where the small truck jumped the curb. And he could stop home for his SUV and make a quick run to the station before the meeting with his siblings. And ask around about Wes Matthews and Capital X while he was there. He should get some photos of Charlize's front yard on his own before he left, just to make certain there were some taken.

For that matter, maybe he should call Blythe Kent. Once he knew that he wasn't...

Footsteps sounded. Light, little clicks against hardwood floor from sandals Charlize was wearing. She'd only been gone a minute or two.

Swinging around he looked at her. Saw the little piece of cardboard between two of her fingers. Glanced back at her face. She'd make a great poker player. Was giving him nothing.

He looked down at her hand again, finding it difficult to draw in a long, healthy breath. Had no personal experience with the stick things. He'd heard of them, of course. Couldn't watch television without knowing some things, but none of his four sisters had had children yet, and...

"So?" he asked when he felt like his brain might explode with needing to know what he was dealing with.

She shrugged. "I don't know yet. You have to wait three minutes." She was expressly not looking at the strip on the stick in her hand.

"How long has it been?"

"However long I've been standing here, minus the thirty seconds it took me to get out here afterward."

He stared at her hand. It was trembling, the little test also shaking. Wouldn't matter if it was in vise grips right in front of his nose, he had no idea how to read results on it.

"Give it to me," he said, reaching out for it. Either she would, or his question would tick her off enough to get her out of the seemingly panicked state she'd apparently fallen into.

She shook her head. "I can handle it just fine," she told him, irritation clearly in her tone. So good, he'd pissed her off. Would distract her from any panic.

After looking at the phone she'd carried out with her, she dropped it back to her side, the stopwatch app he'd seen briefly now facing her skirt. She said nothing.

Apparently, he wasn't privy to the timing.

So they stood there, facing each other from several feet apart. He didn't know about her, but his heart was thumping and he either wanted a beer or to never eat again, depending on which second was ticking past.

When the high beeping sounded from her phone, he felt his entire body tense, though, thankfully, he didn't reach for the gun at his side as he had earlier when the truck had first started careening toward Charlize. He'd been too far away at that point to get a shot off. And later, had only been interested in getting to her, making sure she was okay.

And…she'd glanced at the stick. Quickly. And then again. At which point, she didn't glance away.

What was she trying to do? Kill him?

"Well?" he asked.

He knew, when her gaze met his, what she was going to tell him.

And still felt a blow from the words when she said, "It's positive."

* * *

She'd been worrying about that very moment for weeks. Ten weeks. Every day praying for her period that would tell her she wasn't pregnant. And every night going to bed without it.

The reality of facing this situation was worse than anything she'd imagined.

Never, in her worst nightmare, had she imagined Riley Colton standing in her living room, losing color in the skin she could see above his beard, staring at her as though she'd just told him he had a week left to live.

And yet…she felt oddly…elated, too! Could that be right? Standing there, assessing everything from the outside in, as though she was in the home of one of her clients instead of her own, she checked herself.

Becoming a mother had always been as important to her as finding her one true love. So the latter had proved to be a fantasy that broke her heart—that didn't mean she couldn't thrive on the motherhood part.

A baby!

She had a baby growing inside her! She touched her stomach, feeling warm inside as she let her hand rest over the flatness.

She was going to be a mother…and have a son or daughter of her own!

Oh, God. She had to sit down.

Ramifications flooded her brain in no logical form or order of importance. She'd need a nursery. Aunt Blythe's sewing room? She couldn't ask her aunt to give that up.

Would they have to move? She loved their neighborhood—or had until a pickup had tried to run her over that afternoon. Aunt Blythe had several friends within walking distance.

And… Riley Colton was still there. Standing by the window. His expression seemingly vacant.

Seeing him, a bit of order returned to her existence. She had to get rid of him.

"Why are you here?" He'd said he'd tell her after the test. It was after the test. He needed to say his piece and vacate the premises. And her life.

Her phone rang. An officer was coming by within an hour to take her statement. Riley was answering a text. Looked over at her. "I'm going to head to the station to give my statement," he said. "I'm going to take a few pictures outside first." He moved toward the door.

"Wait a minute!" Just a damned minute. He wasn't walking out on her again.

He turned back. Nodded, though she had no idea what he was agreeing to. Wasn't even sure he knew. The man looked poleaxed. Not to be mean, but she kind of liked that he was suffering a bit after what he'd put her through.

And hated that he was, too. Because that was her way. She cared about people. Felt compassion for them.

"Why were you heading down my street?" she asked.

"We need to talk about…this." He pointed to the basic vicinity of her midsection.

She wanted to refuse, especially since he couldn't have known she was pregnant when he was walking down her street. She wanted to deny him any conversation at all regarding the rest of her life. But knew she didn't have that right. Not ethically. And not legally, either.

"I agree," she said. "And we will, but for right now, it's best if we each get a little space to process. We just found out. Until half an hour ago, you didn't even know of the possibility. Let's think it over, and then talk."

His nod this time was more vigorous. He seemed to almost smile, but with the beard, she couldn't be sure. But she was pretty sure she'd just gotten closer to getting rid of him.

She had plans to make. A doctor's appointment to schedule. Things to think about. She was going to be a mother!

Aunt Blythe would struggle a bit with Charlize not having a husband. As would her parents have if they'd still been alive. Falling in love at first sight, and having that passion last a lifetime, ran in their family like dark hair, long legs and the need to wear glasses. It was up to her, as their only child, to continue the family heritage…

"I'm here to speak with your aunt." Riley's words brought her attention front and center on him. Fully focused.

Huh? "What business do you have with Aunt Blythe?" If he thought he was going to tell her aunt about Charlize's one night of stupidity, well…

He pulled a card out of his back pocket, came close enough to hand it to her.

Aunt Blythe's calling card? She looked at him, frowning. "Where did you get this?"

"I'm working on a case," he said, suddenly alive again, his newly vibrant essence taking over the living room. Filling her with a sense of security and fear at the same time. "My client was suckered into an investment scam. He's out fifty grand. He brought me the brochures he picked up from the seminar he attended and your aunt's card was among them. I'd like to speak with her, to find out what she knows…"

Charlize stepped forward, protective instincts in full gear. "You think she's involved somehow?"

"That's what I need to find out."

"What's the scam?"

"My client invested in a new vitamin that doesn't yet have FDA approval. It was an illegal pyramid scheme…"

Alarm bells rang. "Vitamins?" She didn't care about the legalities of pyramid schemes at the moment. He hadn't even completed a nod before she said, "Revita-You?" Please, let this all be a mix-up.

"You know about them?" His brow creased as his gaze filled with a renewed urgency. "You aren't taking them, are you?"

"Me? No!" And as he visibly relaxed back a space, she asked, "Why?" Feeling not the least bit relieved.

"Because they apparently made my client's girl-friend sick."

Oh, God. She stared at Riley, her heart pounding. "There's a jar of them in my aunt's bathroom. And a case under her bed."

"You think she's taking them herself." It was a state-ment not a question. And based on the jar in the bath-room, she nodded.

"For how long?"

"I noticed them a week ago."

And Aunt Blythe hadn't been feeling well recently. Granted, she'd suffered from migraines most of her adult life, but…

"I asked her about them…she's still really independent when it comes to her rights to her choices so I can only do so much…she said she was trying to turn back time…" she continued. "I didn't like the sound of that, but she said they're only vitamins, nothing prescription, so I wasn't all that worried. Worst case, they were placebos that did nothing."

Riley nodded. "They're supposed to make you look ten years younger within weeks. Or that's the scam that's being sold."

"By who?" She was pissed now. More than pissed.

"That's what I need to find out. I need to speak with your aunt. To find out what she can tell me."

Scared to the bone now, she needed him to be doing better at his job.

"What about your client? Didn't he tell you who's behind this?"

"He's given me everything he has, and we're just in the beginning stages of the investigation," he said, speaking slowly, in a way that made her think he wasn't telling her everything.

Maybe he couldn't. She had to know, anyway. Her mother's two older sisters—Aunt Blythe, and an aunt not far outside Grand Rapids, Gracie—were the only biological family she had left.

"The case just came to me today," he said. "My brother and sisters and I are meeting tonight to discuss our next steps. We're all just collecting what information we can to bring to the table."

She nodded. Gathered herself together enough to know that alienating him at that point was not smart. To realize that she might need his help.

Not with the baby, but…he was a better witness to

what happened to her that afternoon then she'd be… and now this vitamin thing with Aunt Blythe…

She searched her mind for anything she might know that could help him. "Aunt Blythe has been acting kind of jumpy these past couple of days. Absentminded, maybe. Like she could be nervous about something. She wouldn't talk about it, though." She wanted to go straight to the older woman. Get her up and…

"She's out cold when she takes those headache pills," she said aloud. "She's seventy-six years old and while she's still in good mental shape, she gets a bit forgetful when she's upset, and is best after she's rested…"

"That's fine," Riley said, backing up toward the door. "I'll check back with you in the morning. The police are on their way, but are you sure you're okay here alone?" He'd stopped several feet before the door.

"We have a state-of-the-art alarm system, inside and out, and I'll keep my mace and cell phone within reach at all times."

He still hesitated. Frowning. Fearing baby talk, something she absolutely wasn't ready for at that point, she said, "I'm a big girl, Riley. I've been dealing with destructive clients most of my career and am fully trained in self-defence, and capable of looking out for myself."

He nodded. Glanced again at her belly. Opened his mouth as though he was going to say something, closed it again and still didn't leave.

"We'll talk about *it* tomorrow, too," she said softly, her heart reaching out to him. She was a natural at feeling out the needs of others and offering what help she could. It made her good at her job.

"Can I have your cell phone for a second?"

The request was odd, but after pulling it out of the pocket of her dress, she handed it to him. She had nothing to hide.

He pushed the screen a time or two, typed for a second, handed it back to her. "I should have done that three months ago," he said. "My number's there. I keep my cell on, and on me at all times. Call me if there's even a hint of trouble tonight. Or if you think of anything else…"

She wasn't going to call him. Even if there was trouble. She'd dial 911. As was her protocol. But she nodded. Saw him to the door. Locked it behind him.

And then, leaning back against it, let the tears flow.

Chapter 4

Michaela was off shift and had already left when Riley got to the police station. He gave his statement to an officer on hand, and sent the photos he'd taken of Charlize's front yard and sidewalk from his phone to Detective Daniel Gomez, as the detective had instructed. It was possible whoever had almost hit Charlize had been paying attention to his phone, lost control of the car, and didn't want her to report it—the reason for the threat she'd heard. More likely, one of her clients' abusers had been trying to scare her off. Either way, the police had a handle on it.

By the time he got to the house Ashanti had left for the day. Her husband, Jeffrey, was hosting a regional math competition at the high school that night and Ashanti had volunteered to head up the technical security for the event, to prevent cheating.

Brody still wasn't at Riley's house. Wasn't answering his phone. Which pissed Riley off a bit. He tried to hang on to the anger as he fed Pal, and put together a tray of veggies and dip, and another one of various cheeses and meats and crackers to feed his siblings. Brody had a lot of nerve, asking them all to give up time in their lives to help him, and then not showing up.

The anger didn't make it through the first cucumber. The kid was scared to death. Riley hoped to God he was okay.

That Capital X or Wes Matthews hadn't already gotten to him.

But as his brother and sisters gathered in their regular seats at the dining room table, all with folders and electronic tablets, but with no real news to report yet, he looked around at their mostly worried faces and said, "At this point, Capital X needs Brody alive so that they can get their money back. He's got that in his favor."

Everyone was munching off the trays he'd set out. Waiting on Brody, who knew the meeting was at eight. And he was begging them for help. Each of the siblings had their own set of questions for him—all different ways to try and figure out where Wes Matthews was. If he was working alone. Who supplied RevitaYou? And how did Capital X fit into it all?

"I can't say the same for Wes Matthews. If he's afraid Brody's going to talk, or if someone did follow him this morning and they know he's come to us for help…" He shook his head. They were all professionals. Knew the stakes.

A set of twins was on each side of the table, facing

each other, with Griffin on one end and Riley on the other, and all exchanged glances. Just as they'd been doing since they were old enough to occupy those seats at the table. He'd been feeding them all ever since they entered his life. He'd gone from being the only child to nursemaid, babysitter, transporter, teacher, cheerleader, fight monitor, protector and tear wiper—all without anyone asking him what *he* wanted.

His parenting days had been thrust upon him as a young teen, by parents with a social schedule necessary to uphold Graham Colton's political career. They'd hired help, of course. Nannies. Housekeepers. But the girls had always come to him. And his parents had, too, asking him to take up the slack.

Still, the girls were now all grown. As was Griffin, adopted by Graham and Kathleen after the girls were born. Griffin had come with his own set of needs— some of which had been thrust upon Riley. He'd tried his best to be there for his younger brother.

And maybe he hadn't tried hard enough for Brody. By then, he'd already staked a claim on his own life, had been living a life of danger fighting crime as an agent with the FBI.

Riley's parenting days had been long gone for years by then. And good riddance.

He gulped silently. Reached for the bottle of beer he'd brought to the table with him as he remembered his parting words to Charlize the night he'd walked out of that hotel room he'd rented for the two of them. Something about him not being in the market for a relationship, and having zero interest in marriage or children.

It had been completely true then. And was still.

And yet…he was going to be a father? He couldn't wrap his mind around the idea. Had absolutely no intention of letting his siblings know. At least not until he and Charlize talked.

He was going to be financially responsible for his offspring. That was a given.

And it struck him…what if she didn't plan to have the baby? Or keep it? A whole new tension took hold of him. Not in a good way.

How could it have taken him so long to consider that there were other options?

Clearly his brain wasn't in full functioning mode. He was in shock.

Suddenly, the need to know if she wanted to have the child was greater than anything else. He'd assumed she did. Needed to speak with her before she did anything. He had a say, didn't he?

Maybe not.

But if she was going to do something, wouldn't she have taken the pregnancy test sooner? She hadn't had to wait three months.

Easing back into his seat, feeling a bit more relaxed, he looked up to see all five of his siblings staring at him.

"What?"

"Your phone just beeped a text."

Because, of course, they all knew his ringtones for everything. They knew everything about him. Or thought they did.

After picking up the phone, he opened his messaging app. "It's from Brody," he said, "but from a number I don't recognize." And then read aloud,

"I'm safer on my own. Please find Matthews and my money so I can be in Sadie's wedding instead of six feet under."

Damn.

"He's street savvy," Griffin said, looking at the glum faces around the table. He'd finished off half the meat and cheese on his own, with his beer only a quarter gone. "And I'm not sure we should be taking on this case," he continued. "We're all about seeking justice, not finding big sums of money or solving white-collar crimes."

"Brody's seeking justice. He's been scammed," Sadie said. She'd brought in a bottle of beer from the refrigerator, as well.

Griffin scoffed. "Brody's an attorney who most certainly should have known better than to buy into a pyramid scheme, and definitely had to have known the risk in getting involved with a loan shark! Besides, you all know he has no interest in justice. All he cares about is a high-paying corporate job and living the good life."

Griffin had always had a bit of an edge with Brody—maybe tinged by a bit of jealousy—in spite of their similar starts in life. His words also carried a lot of truth.

Flicking a strand of her long dark hair behind her shoulder, Pippa said, "I personally want to see this Wes Matthews guy—banker, con artist, whatever he is—stopped before he can steal the life savings from other people. Besides, we can't let Capital X break every bone in Brody's body. He's family." Her glass of red wine had come from the bottle Riley bought just for her. Anytime it was empty, he replaced it with another just like it.

Her twin, Kiely, sipping the cognac he also kept in stock, nodded beside her.

"Pippa's right, Brody's family. I'll work whatever overtime I have to work to help him," Sadie added.

Vikki took a sip of her sparkling wine. "I'm in on the overtime. Whatever it takes. I think we have to do this."

"Then I'm in," Griffin said, having lost the edge to his tone.

Riley nodded, proud of his siblings, pleased with them. Even Griffin. Every family needed a member that kept them in check.

And he needed them gone so he could call Charlize. Find out if she was planning to keep the baby.

"Since Brody's a no-show, let's all regroup individually tonight..." He handed them each one of the brochures Brody had left. "See what you come up with and meet back here in the morning with a plan. Can you all get here early? I'll make breakfast."

"French toast?" Sadie asked.

"Breakfast wraps." Pippa overrode the choice.

"Just make sure there's plenty of coffee," Griffin said with only a hint of a grumble.

Nodding at all of them as he shooed them out the door, Riley checked the refrigerator to see what he had enough of to make in the morning without having to run to the store.

And then dialed Charlize Kent. He had her number from the call he'd made to himself—and immediately hung up upon—from her phone earlier that evening.

* * *

As soon as her phone rang, Charlize knew who it was. She'd programmed his name into her contacts. And had figured, as soon as she'd seen how he left his number on her phone via her call log, that he'd be contacting her.

She might not have known Riley Colton for long, but she knew he was not a man who was going to be put off when it came to one of his own. What person who'd taken on five siblings as a young teen, and then given up his own career with the FBI to run the family professional investigative service, would turn his back on his own child?

Funny how the things that had drawn her to him that night three months ago, were now the biggest problem she faced.

And funny how she'd forgotten those things about him when she'd convinced herself that she didn't have to contact him about the baby, before she'd known for sure there was one, telling herself that he was a leaver and she couldn't risk him leaving her child.

She let the call go to voice mail.

He might be a man who wouldn't be put off, but she was a woman who wouldn't be bullied. Or coerced. They'd agreed to speak the following morning.

Yeah, and what if he'd been calling about Aunt Blythe? Or had found out something new about the case from his client?

She called him back. Funny, too, how she thought he was a bigger problem than the news she'd confirmed that afternoon. All those weeks dreading taking the test, all the anxiety she currently felt as she faced a completely changed life, and yet, she was happy, too.

She was going to be a mother! Have a baby of her own!

He answered on the fourth ring, though he'd just hung up from calling her, so he couldn't have been that far from his phone.

"You called?" she asked as soon as she heard his voice. He'd have seen her number come up.

"Yes, I…"

"Have more information for me regarding your client and RevitaYou?" The man brought out the snark in her. And her aunt's connection to the vitamins was the only reason he'd initially contacted her.

Another thing not to like about him.

"No. I…just need to ask…"

His hesitancy grabbed at her. "What?" she asked, her tone softening naturally. It was who she was.

"Are you…? You've had a bit of time to think about choices…and…are you planning to have the baby?" The last came out quickly, and with authority. If such a question could carry such a tone.

For the first time she wondered if maybe that tough-guy exterior hid a vulnerability Riley Colton didn't want the world to see.

Then she thought about some of the cases he'd told her about the night that they'd somehow crammed their lives into hours as though they couldn't share enough fast enough. Couldn't get to know each other fast enough.

As though they'd been waiting all of their lives to finally have someone to share it all with.

The train of thought came to an abrupt halt. No more fantasy world for her.

She had a child to think about.

And a man who wanted to know if he was going to be a father, apparently.

"What would your choice be?" she asked as though it mattered. "You're half of this. You have some say."

If he wanted her to not have the baby, could she take that information to court and make sure that he never got parental rights?

Did she want that on record for her child to perhaps find someday?

"I would choose for the child to be born."

Charlize almost dropped the phone as tears sprang to her eyes. She blinked them quickly away. Sat up straight at the table where she'd been sitting with her laptop, looking at nursery furniture.

"It's good to know we agree on something," she said, feeling a smile coming on. And then, even though he couldn't see her but not wanting him to get any false ideas about her being some kind of softie, asked, "Anything else?"

"Have you heard any more from the police?"

"Just that they suspect it could have been an abuser on a case I've worked. It's not the first time I've been threatened, though it's the first time that anything as gutsy as this happened. They're patrolling my place tonight, but all is calm and quiet. Is that all?"

"For tonight."

The words could have been ominous. They sounded more like reassurance. Because she was tired, no doubt.

There was no picture she could come up with where she and Riley Colton sharing a child brought any kind of happiness or peace. No picture where it even worked.

But when she hung up and went back to baby-paraphernalia surfing as a way of distracting herself from the memory of the truck that had almost killed her that night—one of her clients' abusers she felt sure—she had a bit of a smile on her face.

Riley woke Pal as he climbed out of bed before dawn the next morning. He'd been up late doing research on drug production, from creation to government sanctions and approval, to marketing and sales. One thing was clear to him that hadn't been when he'd met with Brody or his siblings the day before. They were missing a vital piece to the puzzle.

The scientist who'd created RevitaYou.

He'd already had a full day of work ahead of him with the two CI cases they were currently working, and had an assignment list for both Ashanti and Bailey, covering aspects of both of those, plus Brody's troubles. Ashanti, a better techie than anyone he'd seen with the FBI, would work from home in the evenings as necessary, and Bailey, who had aspirations of joining the FBI, spent his days wherever it took to track down whatever he might be seeking. If there were physical clues, he'd find them. People, documents, evidence... the same.

What Riley hadn't done was welcome thoughts about diapers. He'd changed a million of them but none in twenty-five years.

Sadie had been three when she'd finally been fully trained. Riley remembered because his mom had insisted that she would be fine in her big-girl panties at his party. She'd been doing okay, but he was just certain she'd have an accident and ruin things. She hadn't. Not that night and never again.

Showered, in black jeans, an off-white polo shirt and

black leather shoes, he dropped the lists on his full-time employees' desks and went in to make breakfast wraps and French toast, put out half and half and plenty of cut-up fruit in a bowl big enough to feed the six of them. Leaving paper plates stacked on the counter so no one got the idea to get real ones down from the cupboard and leave them for him to wash, he stuck a bag of plastic silverware beside them and went into his office to text Charlize. It was his private space—usually respected by all—and he wasn't answering any questions from nosy know-it-alls who'd think they had the right to know who he was texting.

At the moment he was sticking to the case he was about to discuss with his siblings.

Did Blythe invest in RevitaYou? Please let me know ASAP.

By the time he'd joined his siblings at the table, both French toast and breakfast wrap on his plate, and a big mug of coffee in front of him, he still hadn't heard from Charlize.

About anything.

At the moment his focus had to be fully on Brody, whom he hoped to God was safely in hiding. Yeah, the kid was definitely street savvy, and probably still knew some people who could help him stay off the grid, but Capital X was bigger and smarter than Brody Higgins, and they'd made it clear they were after him and weren't fooling around.

Pal wasn't fooling around, either, as she sat at attention, watching the floor around the table for any crumbs. Riley knew it was no mistake the dog always seemed to hang out on Sadie's side of the table.

He started the meeting while everyone was busy chewing, and therefore quiet.

"I want to hear from each of you. Tell me anything you've found out since I first called you yesterday, and then give me a plan," he started, as always. Each member of the CI team had equal say. And responsibility. As the one elected to run the business, he knew his job, in addition to his own investigative work, was to corral them all and keep order. Each sibling would speak when called upon and listen when not, until the reports were done.

"First, here's what I've got, most of which Ashanti emailed to me last night. She found twenty-two investors. There may be more. Three of them appear to have been lured in by Wes Matthews, based on some emails she was able to hack through from an address Brody had for Matthews that has since been deleted. Just as he had with Brody, Matthews passed along promises of financial reward in those emails. And with the first three, there was talk about the dividends they'd received, too. Though we don't yet have bank records to back this up, the first three were paid back double their investment within the two weeks Matthews had promised…"

Kiely, the toughest of her sisters, and not prone to watching what she said, was frowning at him.

"What?"

"Eat," she said, glancing at his untouched plate.

Kind of hard to stomach food when you were busy pushing back against a maelstrom of reaction to the personal news he'd received the night before. He took a sip of coffee.

"There were also three, an apparent second tier, who got back their investment, plus ten grand, paid for, I assume, by the third group. That consisted of the other eighteen, including Brody, who were conned out of fifty grand a piece."

Kiely frowned. He sipped. Popped a piece of banana into his mouth. Picked up the phone he'd purposely left facedown on the table, glanced at the screen for notifications and, finding none, put it back down. "Still nothing from Brody," he announced.

And nothing from Charlize.

"Ashanti found some of the deleted RevitaYou website, which she was able to track down to the app where it was made and stored. Based on that video, the first three investors were paid out of money from the second group, as well as getting their own money back, with the express purpose of unknowingly, we'll assume for now, becoming Matthews's dog-and-pony show. These are the testimonials that Brody talked to me about. The people who spoke at the seminars, assuring everyone that the payback Matthews promised was real."

Kiely's third frown was his warning.

Taking a moment to face his French toast, he put the food into his mouth, chewed, forced the swallow—all to keep his siblings from jumping into his shorts. The downside to having five top-rate investigators sitting at your table.

"I pulled up profiles on social media, and it looks like the testimonials of the RevitaYou users shown in the video, and at the live seminars, exist, as well. They're regular people with long-standing accounts posting family vacations, holiday memories and pictures of the food they're eating."

And that, unfortunately, was about all he had to give them.

Unless he unloaded his diaper woes, which he absolutely was not going to do.

Except...

"I've made contact with one RevitaYou user." Blythe was maybe more than just a user, but her possible involvement didn't go into the report until he knew what he had to report. "I'll be following up with her as soon as we're done here. And I've left a list of the others who are local for Bailey to track down when he gets in."

Everyone nodded at him, most with empty paper plates in front of them. Vikki got up for more coffee. Filled her siblings' cups, as well. All ceramic—off the mug tree his mother had always kept on the kitchen counter. Hopefully, they'd all be in the dishwasher, too, before everyone left.

"I checked the paper used for the brochures," Sadie said, out of turn, but she had everyone's attention. "It's the most common brand, used by pretty much every printer in the city. So far, there's nothing there that I can use to trace it to anything in particular. It's digitally printed, which leaves fewer clues than, say, if it had been typeset, where we might get a particular smudge or chip, something that could lead us to one particular plate. I also tried to dust for prints on the one you gave me, ran the clear ones I could get through my databases, and got nothing."

"So we can assume this Matthews hell monger is relatively new to the game?" Kiely asked. "Which would explain why I came up with nothing on him." As a PI freelancing with local and national agencies, Kiely had some unique sources.

"Eighteen people are out fifty grand each?" Griffin shook his head, the blond hair combed just right even that early in the morning, a grim look in his green eyes. "I know someone who got mixed up in Capital X, tried to contact him last night, but haven't heard back yet. I'll make it my top priority today."

Riley looked at Pippa, who was next in line around the table. "I know an attorney who has a boutique firm in the building where Brody works. I've asked her to get me the surveillance footage from yesterday. I should have it later today and hopefully we'll at least have a description for the Capital X goons."

"I can run them through facial recognition once you've got them," Sadie piped in again, and then looked at Riley. "You should try to connect with Detective Emmanuel Iglesias to see if anyone else has complained or reported in about Matthews or RevitaYou. He'd be the one who'd most likely know."

"And I'll see what I can find on Wes Matthews, if there's anything in the banking world about him. That should give us a starting point, if nothing else," Kiely added.

"I'm going to scour military justice records for any mention of Capital X, and ask around to see if anyone from JAG knows anything about them or has any leads," Vikki said, her expression as straight as her long blond hair. "I have to believe, since they were on FBI radar, that we've come up against them, too."

"Okay, that's it—everyone off to work and keep in touch," Riley said, scooping food into his mouth as he stood with his plate. And then, as the sun coming in the window hit a sharp glint off from the diamond on Sadie's left hand, he had to ask, "How are the wedding plans coming?" The other four stopped, all in various stages of gathering their stuff and leaving the table, and looked over at their sister, her shoulder-length blond hair framing the smile on her face.

"Good!" she said. "Tate's been gone a lot, so I'm doing most of the work, but that way I get to make all the choices!" She grinned, seemingly unaware that not a single one of her siblings liked the businessman she'd fallen head over heels in love with.

Riley's gut clenched. He wanted Sadie happy. Wished all of the Coltons would find partners to cook for them and give them families so he could live in peace. There was just something about Tate Greer that didn't sit right with him. He'd checked the guy out himself, though, and found nothing on him, so said, "If you need any help, let one of your sisters know."

Which brought up a chorus of halfhearted offers from the other three Colton women in the room.

And it dawned on him—all four of them were going to have another big event in their lives, probably before Sadie became a wife. They were going to be aunts, and Griffin an uncle.

And he dreaded the moment he was going to have to tell them.

Dreaded the shocked looks he knew he'd see, followed by the doubt in his abilities to suddenly become a father at forty-three. Dreaded disappointing them.

He was, after all, the head of the family.

For whatever that was worth.

Chapter 5

She wasn't texting him until she'd had a chance to speak with her aunt about the vitamins herself. Charlize had made the decision sometime in the night, during one of the several times she'd woken and lain there in the dark with her mind careening from place to place. Problem to problem. Situation to situation. Counting the hours that passed safely. And always coming back to the baby growing inside her. And the man who'd fathered it.

The *night* he'd fathered it.

That evening had started out as a dream come true for her. Or rather, a reality finally coming to pass. She'd found her true love.

Growing up with a mother who jumped in and out of relationships because she never waited for love, Charlize was most influenced by her mother's parents and aunts who often watched her when her mother was off on another fling. Her grandmother had introduced her to romance novels as a teenager, telling her not to settle for less than the real thing, and she often talked about how she knew she was going to marry her grandfather the night she met him. And he always claimed he knew she was the one for him the first night they met. Aunt Gracie and Uncle Fred had also been together since high school.

Aunt Blythe would tell her it didn't always happen that way, though. She'd also had her true love, who'd died in an accident weeks before they were married, and she'd never met anyone who could take his place. She would tell the story of how they'd been friends all through high school, went to different colleges and reconnected six years later. Both her aunts and her grandmother stressed that the reason for Charlize's mother's unhappiness and eventual death from chemical abuse was due to her rushing to find what her mother and older sisters had had, rather than waiting for the right man to come along. She hadn't even known who'd fathered her one and only child.

For thirty years Charlize had been waiting diligently, but had never met a man who felt like her other half until the night she met Riley Colton. She hadn't been looking that night. To the contrary, she'd been preoccupied with the All Welcome fundraiser—had been focused on the amount of money needed to build the community center—when Riley started talking to her.

But she'd been hooked by the sound of his voice. The way, the first time he'd looked her in the eye, her stomach had jumped. And then settled.

For a few hours she'd had heaven on earth. Until

she'd realized she'd been like a kid at a theme park, living in a fantasy world that, behind the scenes, wasn't all that pretty.

And now she was entering fantasyland again—for real this time—becoming a mother. And would forever be aware of a less beautiful existence behind the scenes, too, in the form of the baby's father.

He just didn't fit. Not in her life. Not in any of the plans she needed to make...

Her phone rang just as she was heading back to her aunt's bedroom, to check in on her, maybe wake her up. Grabbing the cell on the first ring, she hurried back out to the kitchen where she'd squeezed fresh orange juice and was ready to make Blythe's oatmeal.

She'd already called to have another private practice social worker cover her two in-home visits that morning.

She recognized the number, but it wasn't Riley Colton's.

"Laurene, what's up?" she asked as soon as she could speak without fear of having her aunt be privy to the conversation. Business was confidential, even from home.

"Ronny's real mad," her client said, almost at a whisper, and every nerve in Charlize's body stood on end. Having been appointed by the court to counsel Laurene and ostensibly Lonny, too, to keep contact with the household, Charlize was trying to help Laurene Dill get a better job so that she could afford to leave her emotionally abusive boyfriend.

"Is he there?" First and foremost, she had to look out for the twenty-year-old's safety.

"No. I just… I don't know if he…you know…has sound on the cameras he's got around…"

The home security system she'd found installed at the house and had added to her notes after yesterday's home visit. Twenty-four-year-old Ronny Simms had dangerously serious jealousy issues. Laurene claimed that Ronny had never hit her, though he'd threatened to more than once, but he was high up on the police radar just the same—and as of the previous week, in the court system, as well. On four different occasions, neighbors had dialed 911 for drunk and disorderly conduct and damaging others' property. During the last incident, Ronny had stubbed his toe on a painted rock acting as a doorstop then thrown it out a window of their home. It had sailed the small distance between their house and the house next door, breaking a window.

The doorstop had been a gift to Laurene from a high school friend with whom she was no longer in touch. Ronny hadn't liked it in their home from the beginning, then had blamed Laurene for his damaged toe. The police had arrested him, charges had been filed and he'd been sentenced the week before to six months of probation and anger management classes. The court had also ordered the services of a social worker for the home.

Which was why Charlize was on the case. She was to monitor the home for signs of abuse. And to counsel members of the household in terms of healthy living. After speaking with Laurene in private the day before, Charlize's theory was that Ronny was jealous of, or feeling threatened by, whatever feelings Laurene still had for her friend. That, more than the physical pain, had launched the attack that had landed him in jail. He'd not only broken a window, he'd also thrown everything he could get his hands on in the kitchen where the doorstop had been sitting along the wall.

"He just kept going on and on about your visit yesterday," Laurene was saying, her quiet desperation setting off Charlize's internal warning bells.

"What he's doing to you isn't right," Charlize said, her tone filled with the strength of her belief. It could take years to undo the emotional and mental damage Ronny had done to Laurene, but first and foremost, they had to break through the manipulation enough to get the young woman out from under his control. "You know that. That's why you talked to me, why you're filling out the job applications I brought you. Why we're working on your interview skills." She'd repeat the words a thousand times if that was what it took.

And in her experience, sometimes it took every single one of those repetitions.

And sometimes it still didn't work.

But for the ones it helped…the ones who managed to break free…to regain control of their minds, their lives…

"You shouldn't have to hide in the closet and talk in a near whisper just to make a phone call," she continued when Laurene remained silent. "You're a grown, capable, loving woman. You have every right to decide who you want to speak to, and you certainly have every right to speak to your court-appointed advocate."

"How do you know I'm in a closet? Are you watching me, too?"

If she wasn't as well trained as she was, Charlize would have teared up at that. "Of course not, Laurene.

It's not normal to live with cameras on you all the time, with someone watching every move you make. Home security systems are intended to watch your home when you're away..." Or to keep an eye on an offender in your home, perhaps, in extreme cases, but she was not going to cloud Laurene's already confused mind with extraneous details. "I noticed the cameras when I did my initial walk-through yesterday. He's got them in every room, including the bathroom, which is very not normal. He's watching you more carefully in that house than you'd be watched in prison."

Because Ronny had her in a prison of his own making.

"He just wants to make sure I'm safe," Laurene said. "We don't live in a great neighborhood. There's a lot of crime here. And he loves me so much. He worries about me, about something happening to me. I don't think he'd make it without me. If you knew the way he grew up, the things that happened...he never knew about love and compassion until he met me."

The words could be beautiful...if Charlize didn't recognize the rhetoric. The things Ronny had told Laurene were probably true. As true as the fact that he had real problems, abusive tendencies, surely resulting from his youth, but still illegal. Abusive.

And the courts had determined that he posed a risk to Laurene's life.

"He wants to be able to call 911 immediately if anyone breaks in."

"Then he's not going to like you being in the closet for the length of this phone call," Charlize said, worried that Ronny was going to commit serious physical harm before she could be successful in getting the other woman out of that environment.

"I told him that I have to have time to pray in privacy, and he said I could use the closet." She supplied the information as though there was nothing at all odd about it. "And I'm using the phone you gave me so he can't see the call on our records."

Thank God Laurene had told her that Ronny checked her calls regularly or she wouldn't have known to provide a preloaded phone. And thank God double that Laurene was actually using the phone.

It meant that maybe Laurene had some doubts where Ronny's behavior was concerned. That she was at least listening a little bit.

It meant there was hope.

"Do you pray often?" she asked, wanting to know how much Laurene was using her only escape route.

"Every day. I come in here anytime I just need some time to myself, you know?"

"So you aren't really praying."

"No, it's just what I could think of that wouldn't make Ronny feel...you know...agitated. He likes it that I pray."

A grown woman, trapped in a closet for moments of personal freedom, lying about praying just to get those moments, and she couldn't see...

Charlize wished the blindness was an anomaly, something that was shocking and...fixable. Preventable. Unfortunately, it was an everyday occurrence. One in four women were victims in some fashion and...

"He was...really...agitated...last night," the younger woman said, a new urgency entering her voice. "He just kept going on and on about you being there, about you messing with my head, messing things up. I just… you can't come back here, Ms. Kent."

"It's court ordered…" she started.

"Then you have to talk to the court," Laurene interrupted, sounding stronger now. "You have to tell them that you came here and we're fine. You can't come back here again."

Sadness filled her as she heard Laurene's strength return only when she was fighting for herself to stay in the prison Ronny had created.

She heard someone moving around, a door closing. Aunt Blythe was up, in the bathroom.

Slipping out the back door to continue her conversation in private, she said, "I can't lie to the court, Laurene. You aren't fine. The things I saw…look at you right now, standing in a closet…"

"I'm not standing. I'm sitting. And…you don't understand. He threatened me, Ms. Kent. Either I convince you we're fine or…he doesn't know what he's going to do. He…raised his fist to me last night. For the first time ever. It's not him. Not my Ronny. You have to stop coming here."

Charlize turned to complete stone for the moment, bracing her mind against the images of distorted faces and abused bodies she'd seen over the course of her job. Then she asked, "Did he hit you?"

"No. He stopped as soon as he saw the horror on my face. But…he was so upset. Who knows what…"

She didn't doubt that Ronny believed he loved Laurene. A lot of abusers loved their prey. And their mental or emotional instabilities tainted that love an ugly color. Her job was to try to teach loved ones how to love and cohabitate in a healthy manner.

Or, as in Laurene's case, to give the young woman means to escape someone like Ronny, who didn't want help.

"I have to make weekly in-home visits," she said softly, but firmly. "If I don't do it, the court will appoint someone else. It's either that, or Ronny could go to jail. These visits were part of the sentencing that kept him out of prison, remember?"

Laurene's silence wasn't reassuring.

"We're all just looking out for you, you realize that, right?"

Nothing.

"I know you're scared, Laurene. That's why I'm here, and will always help in any way I can."

"You just don't know Ronny. I've never seen him as mad as he was last night…"

And it clicked. Right then. Getting herself out of work mode, and Laurene's life, and popping back to her own for a brief second, Charlize thought about the previous night. About the sidewalk and the glint of metal coming at her.

Ronny and Laurene's case hadn't included a police escort stipulation. She'd given the cops their names the evening before, because they'd asked for the names of every client she'd seen recently, but she hadn't thought…

"Does Ronny drive a small black pickup?" she asked.

Laurene's continued silence was not a good sign. Not for Laurene. And not for Charlize, or the baby she was carrying.

Riley was standing in the doorway to the kitchen, marveling at the spotlessly clean counters and sink his siblings had left behind after he'd excused himself from their goodbyes to take a call in his office, when his phone buzzed again.

A text from Charlize. Her aunt was up, having breakfast, and since she was sharpest first thing in the day, Riley should probably head over.

Leaving Pal to welcome Bailey and Ashanti to their day's task lists, he was ringing Charlize's bell within ten minutes of her text. She answered right away, glancing toward his blue SUV parked at the curb, rather than at him.

The visit wasn't personal; he read into that look. They wouldn't be discussing anything close to parenthood or having children, just Blythe.

Which was fine by him.

For the moment.

His body didn't get the memo. It attempted to stand at attention as he took in Charlize, who wore her regular clothes—light blue cotton pants, white short-sleeved tailored blouse and sandals—so seductively in front of him. Professional and yet…more, too.

He was all business, though, when he saw the older woman seated at the table, spooning oatmeal into her mouth, while focused on the tablet in front of her. He caught the online Scrabble game she was playing before she turned the thing off.

And saw some of Charlize in her smile when she shook his hand as they were introduced.

"Mind if I sit down?" he asked, pulling out a chair perpendicular to her at the kitchen table.

She offered him coffee. Charlize asked if he'd eaten. And he got straight to the point, shaking his head in response to their queries.

"I'm a professional investigator, Ms. Kent," he said, taking a seat. "I need to talk to you about RevitaYou."

Blythe's wrinkled brow furrowed as she set down her spoon.

"I found your calling card in a brochure," he said. "Do you have any idea how it came to be there?"

She nodded, looking only at him, as though her niece, who'd taken a seat across from her, wasn't in the room.

"I went to a seminar," she said. "A friend down the street was talking about this poster she'd seen. At first, I was just interested because I wanted to look younger…" She pointed to her face. "These wrinkles and sags…they're so depressing. I used to be quite a pretty woman," she told him, nodding.

"I think you still are," he replied—meaning the words. She didn't look twenty, but her hair was stylish, curly; she was all done up nice, with clothes that made her appear as though she was heading out for a lunch date. And she looked him straight in the eye. That was the icing on the cake for him.

She lifted a hand, knocked against the spoon in her bowl and then used her napkin to clean up the oatmeal she'd spilled.

"So you went to the seminar…" he prompted as she wiped.

"And when I got there, everyone was so excited. Not just the people on stage, but everyone. We were part of something brand-new. And huge. All these people around me, they were talking about how this was a chance they couldn't miss, talking about helping out their families, being able to travel again… I've always wanted to go to Ireland," she said. "Anyway, I had my life savings sitting there, waiting for me to get too frail to take care of myself, waiting to be sucked up by an old folks' home…"

"Aunt Blythe! There's no way you're going to… you'll always have a home with me," Charlize blurted out. Riley glanced her way, saw the wealth of concerned love on her face as she looked at her aunt.

The older woman nodded. "I just didn't want to be a burden on you," she said.

"Did you get return on your investment?" Riley asked before they could segue too far off into family and living arrangements.

He had a child on the way whose living arrangements would coincide with the Kents'. And…his? Possibly? On weekends? Or something?

The thought made him sweat. Profusely.

Blythe rescued him with a slow shake of her head. "I gave Mr. Matthews fifty thousand dollars, and then he stopped returning my calls. The last time I called, the number had been disconnected. But Mr. Matthews was so nice, and I just kept hoping something had gone wrong with his phone and that when he could, he'd get in touch with me."

She was back to looking at only Riley. Leaning toward him, with a shoulder to Charlize. And by the look in those old eyes, he was pretty sure the woman knew full well she'd been had.

"Why didn't you tell me?" Charlize asked softly. Riley had to hand it to her. There was no judgment in her tone. No blame. Just that same concern.

Her voice drew you right in, that mixture of caring and protection. A permanent "have your back" type thing. Could easily become addictive. He'd known that kind of love once. Briefly. With a member of his FBI team…

"You're so busy," Blythe said with a quick glance at Charlize, and then, to Riley, "I was too embarrassed to tell anyone," she said softly. "I'd come across as the batty old woman who'd been an easy mark…"

"My client, who was also an investor, and who had your card in his brochure, is only twenty-seven," he told her. "This has nothing to do with age."

Her gaze sharpened. "I like you, Mr. Colton."

He was beginning to like her, too. This…this… woman who was going to be a great-aunt to his child.

Oh, Lord.

"Did you also buy some vitamins for yourself?" he asked, needing to stick to what he did well—work.

"I bought a case to sell," she said. "They're under my bed. They sell them to the team for thirty dollars a bottle, and then we're to sell them for fifty."

"How many have you sold?" How many people did they need to warn?

"None." She shook her head. "I'm taking them myself, first, just to make sure they work. I've been taking them for five days, and so far…nothing." She flipped a hand to her chin.

"You have to stop taking them," Charlize butted in again.

"They made my client's girlfriend sick." Riley backed her up as Blythe looked between the two of them. Or maybe Brody's girlfriend had ingested something else bad around the time she took the vitamins. But generally, food poisoning would pass. According to Brody, the last time they'd spoken, she was still sick.

Blythe shook her head, looking shocked. "The scientist who created the formula for the vitamins was at the seminar! I talked to him myself. He was smart, you know…talked like a doctor, and gave us a slide show of the components and how they react together, explaining how they work."

"You met the scientist?" he asked, on full alert. A key part Brody had left out the morning before, but then they hadn't had a lot of time to talk before the kid had cut town. With two recently broken fingers, Brody probably wasn't thinking a whole lot about chemical compounds.

"Yes." Blythe nodded. "Yes, I did. Dr. something…" She frowned. "I don't remember his name…"

Filled with new urgency, Riley leaned in closer, needing to get as much as he could out of Blythe before the woman got too tired. If only Brody had shown up the night before…they could very well be much further along on their quest to help him! "Can you describe him to me?" he asked, tempering his tone and willing himself to be calm. Unthreatening.

"He was tall, a lot taller than me, anyway." Blythe spoke slowly, as though trying to recall details. "Kind of white hair, you know like blond and gray mixed. And…blue eyes," the woman finished emphatically.

"You remember the color of his eyes?"

"Because of the glasses he wore." She nodded, clearly confident. "They were silver and wire-rimmed. I remember because the silver was like some of the gray in his hair and I wondered if maybe it would be a good color on me, that silver. Anyway, I kept looking at the glasses and his eyes were right there. I remember the blue because they were a pretty color. Like a girl's."

While he didn't get the connection in the last state-

ment, since a lot of men had blue eyes, Riley was convinced that the woman was remembering something
real, and asked, "Do you have any idea how old he
was?"

Blythe shook her head. "A lot younger than me,"
she said. "Unless it was the vitamins. But the gray in
his blond hair seemed natural, not like he colored it,
so probably not old enough yet to have a full head of
gray hair."

He didn't want her believing that shady vitamins
were going to make anyone look younger. Didn't want
the allure to persuade her to keep taking them.

For her. For Charlize. And for the unborn baby this
woman was surely going to love.

"Those vitamins, you know they aren't FDA ap-
proved," Riley reminded, stating what Brody said he'd
been told at the seminar. "And as far as I can tell, there
are about eighteen of you who are out the total investment."

"I can't believe this!" Charlize stood, walked to the
end of the table, grabbed the back of the chair so tight
he could see white knuckles. "We've got to find this
guy. To get everyone's money back!"

He hadn't really planned on the "we" part. Not even
a little bit.

"I'm going to the police," Charlize said then, giving the top of the chair an ungentle slap. "I'm going to
report this guy…"

"I'm on my way there now," Riley heard himself
admit. "I've got an appointment in half an hour to
speak with a detective…"

Alone. The conversation was planned between him
and Emmanuel Iglesias. Just the two of them.

"I'd like to come with you," Charlize said. "I actually was planning to stop in at the station this morning, anyway. Dealing with a case from work," she said, giving him a pointed look.

Something to do with the near hit and run on her front sidewalk the afternoon before. He knew it without her saying another word. And the more he could have her with him, protecting her and the child, the better he'd feel.

"Then let's go," he said, turning back to her aunt. "Thank you very much, Ms. Kent. You've been extremely helpful. I'm going to do everything I can to get your money back."

She nodded. Got up from the table and took her bowl in hand. "You're a nice man," she said again, heading to the sink.

Riley wondered if she'd still think that about him when her niece told him that he'd knocked her up and then walked out on her.

He was guessing not.

Chapter 6

Grabbing her purse, Charlize didn't argue when Riley said he'd drive. He was agreeing to let her be involved in his conversation with Detective Iglesias, and she knew when to pick her battles—or let them go.

"Has your team been able to find out anything?" she asked as she pulled open the front door, the sound of running water in the distance as Aunt Blythe did up the few dishes left from breakfast.

"We need to talk about the baby."

Shocked, she paused for a second, her hand on the doorknob. Oh, so he was ready to talk now?

The snarky thought was followed by, what had changed? The night before, he couldn't have made it more obvious that the parenthood topic was abhorrent to him.

To be fair…she'd had ten weeks to think about the possibility. He'd had ten minutes.

And his call the night before…

His choice had been to have the baby…as opposed to not.

"I agree," she said, pulling open the door. "We do. I'm just not sure at this point what to say. I'm having the baby. It's yours, too. And we're still virtual strangers."

She threw the last remark over her shoulder as she stepped outside—and caught a way-too-sexy look in those dark eyes as he said, "Oh I wouldn't say strangers. From what I remember we got to know…"

The rest was cut off as a loud crack sounded, followed by a thud and the sound of brick shattering to her right. Something had punctured the wall to the right of her front door.

In shock, staring out toward where the initial bang had come from, she saw a smallish black truck speeding away. Her gaze went to the license plate. The cop she'd spoken to the night before had asked repeatedly if she'd caught any part of the plate.

There was none…

A hand gripped her arm, pulling her back inside the house. It seemed like minutes had passed since she'd taken a step outside. In reality, it had only been a couple of seconds.

"Someone just…" She couldn't believe it. Was shaking, but not consciously afraid. Just… "Someone just shot at me."

Riley was already on the phone. Speaking to Iglesias, based on the greeting. So he had a direct line to the man…

Aunt Blythe. Had her aunt heard the noise?

Charlize heard a toilet flush. Surmised her aunt had no idea what was going on. Wasn't sure what to tell her. She'd been so upset over being scammed…

Plus, the baby on the way…which was going to be a real shock…and probably a disappointment, too. A big one. Charlize was more her mother than her grandmother and aunts after all. They'd tried so hard, had such hope. And she'd let them down…

Which was what she needed to be worrying about right then. Internal sarcasm brought her mind back to the man standing a foot away from her, explaining in greater detail than she'd catalogued, what had just happened. He'd noticed a white driver, male, dark hair.

"Okay, Detective, thank you," Riley was saying.

Her knees felt a little weak. She waited by the door. Wanting to be gone before her aunt reappeared.

"Change of plans," Riley said. "Iglesias is coming here."

She supposed that made sense.

They moved into the living room. She had to sit down. Was feeling a little nauseated. She hadn't thrown up in years. Not since the one time she'd had too much to drink in college.

There was probably a slug in the wall of her house that would need to be removed. Or on the ground close by.

Footsteps sounded and Aunt Blythe appeared in the archway between the living and dining rooms, a purse over her arm. "Oh! I thought you'd left!"

Did the purse mean her aunt was leaving? Charlize looked toward Riley. Was it safe for Blythe to go?

The truck had sped off. The bullet had clearly been meant for her. And that put her baby in danger, too!

"We're having our meeting here," Riley said, walking toward her aunt. "I hope that doesn't disturb any plans you have…"

"It's my bridge morning," she said. "We're playing at Madge's today, down on the corner."

Bridge morning. Every Wednesday. Charlize had completely forgotten. Which showed how much she was off her mark.

"If you don't mind, I'd like to walk down with you," he said, taking her aunt's elbow. "I've got a couple of more questions regarding the vitamins…"

Charlize was pretty sure he didn't, that he'd asked everything he'd had to ask, but when he glanced back at her, his brows raised as though asking if she'd be okay, she nodded, handing him her keys to get back in when he returned. "I'm going to use the restroom," she said, taking her mace out of her purse and showing it to him as she headed to the back of the house. She then sat on top of the toilet, wondering if she was going to puke as she awaited his return.

Loving how he'd stepped right up to help her protect her aunt.

And telling herself not to make too much of it. She and the baby could have been killed. Even if she'd survived, she could have lost her child.

That was where her focus needed to stay.

Not on the man who'd accidentally fathered the life growing inside her.

Riley was great in the moment.

And when the moment was over, he'd be gone.

* * *

The entire way down the block, Riley kept his back between the street and Blythe Kent's back. He could see ahead of them, and to both sides. He had the older woman covered.

He filled the time by asking Blythe if she remembered a young attorney at the seminar, a new investor just like her. And experienced an odd swell of pride as Blythe responded exuberantly about the person who'd been so kind to her, sitting with her on a break, bringing up the RevitaYou website on his phone and explaining the numbers to her. Writing them down on a napkin. And knew a huge spark of guilt, too. If not for Brody's kindness, the older woman might not have been swindled out of a portion of her life's savings.

As soon as Blythe was safely in the house down the street, he hightailed it back to Charlize, coming in the door to an empty living room. A shard of fear shot through him.

"Charlize?" he called. And heard what sounded like a choking sound coming from farther back in the house.

Heading quickly in the direction he'd seen her headed as he left, he heard the sound again—coming from a closed door farther down the hallway. He was reaching for the door handle when he heard the toilet flush. His hand dropped, but he didn't retreat. Perhaps he should have.

But a memory came to him, so clear it could have been recent…him as a teen, holding a toddler on each hip, hearing his mother puking her guts out…

Water was running behind the door, then came the sound of an electric toothbrush. And he knew.

"A cold washcloth to the face helps," he said to the closed door and then made his way to the kitchen, where he opened cupboards until he found a box of saltines. Taking an open container of crackers and a glass of water with him, he made it to the living room at the same time she did.

"I'm sorry," he said, handing her the water and crackers. She took them, put them on the end table as she sat in an armchair perpendicular to the couch.

"Is it happening a lot?" He had to ask.

"I'm sorry you had to hear that," she said, not meeting his gaze. "And no, that was a first. I'm sure brought on by having a bullet fly by me." She seemed to be trying to make light of both the violent morning sickness, and the attempt on her life, too.

He couldn't do the same.

"Crackers help. If you can get them down before you get sick, a lot of times they can ease the nausea."

She looked at him then, kind of frowning, but seeming interested, too. He liked the look. Too much.

"For a guy who's been single all his life and who is adamant about the fact that marriage and children have been forever off the table, you sure know a lot about pregnancy. You got something you need to tell me, Riley?"

Like what? She thought he'd lied to her? He shook his head. But couldn't really blame her for wondering if everything he'd told her had been one big pick-up line.

And couldn't blame her for wanting to talk about something other than the shot that had been taken at her.

"My mom was sick every single afternoon for weeks when she was pregnant with Sadie and Vikki," he confided. That baby she was carrying was going to have aunts. A somewhat confusing slew of them. And an uncle, too.

And maybe Iglesias would get there, allowing him to procrastinate that eventuality a little bit more.

Maybe the man would get there and find out who wanted Charlize out of the way. The fact that the hit hadn't been professional was his only consolation at the moment. If the guy had been any good at all, he wouldn't have missed.

Unless the shot had just been another warning…

"You have twin sisters?" she asked. He'd told her he and his siblings had a firm together, but that had been it. Mostly he'd talked about his career with the FBI that night. Talked about things he never told anyone. He still wasn't sure why.

"Two sets of them, actually," he told her, and then glanced at her stomach. "I hope I didn't pass on the trait…"

With a hand on her stomach, she glanced down, and then back over at him. Their eyes met, but he couldn't come up with anything to say. Neither could she apparently, as she eventually reached for a cracker and asked, "You have two sets of twin sisters?"

He nodded. Had long ago grown used to people's initial reactions when he was out with his siblings—he'd had a ton of practice during the years he'd been at home, helping to raise them. And later, too, when he'd step in for his folks or leave the office if he wasn't out on a case to pick them up from school or some practice or another.

"Both sets are fraternal," he added. "They all look different. No problem telling them apart."

"And you remember your mom getting sick?"

He nodded.

"How old were you?"

Her interest was as focused, as compelling, as he'd remembered. And he found himself opening his mouth to answer, where, for anyone else, he'd have prevaricated, distracted, or even just shrugged.

The conversation itself was a distraction from the possible danger that awaited her outside her front door. They were going to have to deal with that.

"Thirteen for Pippa and Kiely. The morning sickness was really in the morning then, and not that often. At least not that I knew. I was fifteen when she had the other two... She told me about the crackers and water, and cold washcloth. With a toddler on each hip, I always had them ready after that first time."

"You had a child on each hip?"

He nodded. Feeling inept all over again as he remembered some of the other times he hadn't known what to do. Like the time he'd been seventeen, driving the family's huge SUV with four car seats, and Sadie, who'd been two, had suddenly started spewing vomit all over herself. It was the first time she'd thrown up like that and it had been hellacious. She'd been crying, which made Pippa cry, while the other two just leaned forward in the chairs, watching him. He'd pulled into an alcove and called his mom, practically in tears himself.

He must have puking on his mind...

"I was two when you were fifteen," she said slowly. "I could have been one of those toddlers."

He shook his head. "Believe me, they're all grown

up now and a pain in my ass most days." He told it like it was.

"These are the siblings you work with," she said, munching on a cracker.

He nodded. "And there's Griffin. My folks adopted him."

"And you're all in business together." She seemed to be stuck on that for some reason.

"The other five have full-time jobs," he said.

"You say you aren't a family man…"

"I'm not," he quickly inserted. He hadn't lied to her, and couldn't start, either. Especially not now that they were going to have to figure out how he'd take responsibility for the child she carried, do his part, without being a father. If nothing else, he was just too damned old, like a dog learning new tricks. Except for him it would be a dog having to go back through puppy training. He'd done it all. And had no desire to go through it another time.

He was remembering, again, how long it had been since he'd changed a diaper, when she said, "It sounds to me like you're not only a family man, but you're the head of an incredible group of siblings to whom you've devoted your life…"

He shook his head. She had it all wrong. His life had been devoted to the FBI for more than twenty years. He'd only built Colton PI after his folks had died and…

He was saved from trying to explain—to ensure that she saw him as he truly was—by the knock on the door.

Iglesias had arrived.

Gathering up the crackers and water, Charlize carried them into the kitchen as Riley answered the door.

She needed a second to get her head out of fantasyland and back into gear. No point in romanticizing about the ex–FBI agent who'd fathered her child.

He'd walked out on her—not kindly. And actions spoke a whole lot louder than words.

Still, as she walked back into the living room, holding out a hand to the tall, muscular detective who'd just arrived, she couldn't help picturing a younger Riley with a two-year-old on each hip.

Couldn't help feeling a tad bit of love for that picture.

Or for the way Riley met her gaze as she came back into the room, as though asking if she felt okay. She nodded, just in case the question had been there, between them, and felt another twinge of…not hate… at his slight nod back as they took seats—her back in her chair, and the two men on either end of the couch.

Iglesias pulled out a notebook, jotting things as they both told him about the hit and run the day before, naming who, from the GRPD they'd spoken to.

"My understanding was that Gomez was taking on the case," Riley finished.

Iglesias shrugged. "I'll talk to him, request the case. Makes sense that I take this on."

"Good." Riley nodded. "Sadie said you were the one…"

Charlize had no reason to feel more confident in the man, just because of Riley's approval, but she felt more like she was in good hands, just the same.

"Sadie's a character," Iglesias said. "I was surprised to hear that she's marrying Tate Greer. Can't say I've ever liked the man. Just something about him seems kind of off. He's a little too perfect. Too shiny."

Riley's frown made Charlize more curious than an

outsider should have been. "I'm not sure I do, either," he said.

As Iglesias went outside, got an evidence kit from his car and took the bullet out of the wall of her home, after taking photos, Charlize excused herself to the kitchen and another dose of crackers.

Feeling nothing like herself.

Nothing in her life was normal. Her aunt had lost her savings, her life was in danger and she'd just found out she was pregnant. All within a day.

She almost slid down to the floor under the weight of it all.

At a time when, considering the child who was dependent upon her, she had to be stronger than she'd ever been before.

She couldn't afford to feel needy. To be tempted by the chance to rely on someone else.

It was Riley Colton's fault. Whenever he was around, she wasn't herself.

He made her weak.

And so, as soon as this RevitaYou business was settled, he had to go.

Her baby was counting on her.

But…wouldn't it be…nice…if her baby could grow up with the same loving care Riley Colton had been bestowing on his sisters all his life?

Forget nice…it would be a miracle.

And she no longer believed in those.

Because of him.

No way was she going to give him the chance to lead her child into thinking she or he was loved, just to have him walk out on them.

No way in hell.

Chapter 7

Riley assessed Charlize's face the second she walked back into the room to ascertain whether or not her morning sickness had fully passed, just as he'd long ago learned to do with his mother.

Charlize's pinched look was gone. But she avoided his gaze.

He didn't blame her. The night they'd had sex, she'd offered a condom, but he'd had his own, which he'd insisted on using. Always had. He replaced the one in his wallet each week. Knew they were the best money could buy.

He'd had no reason, or thought, to follow up afterward, to make certain there'd been no consequence from the night he'd been trying to forget ever since.

He frankly hadn't even considered that there'd be

one. As far as he knew, he hadn't had a condom fail-ure in the decades he'd been using them.

Iglesias, who was back on his end of the couch, was asking Charlize if she had any idea who wanted her dead. She told him about the list of clients she'd given to the officer who'd come to the house the night be-fore. He wanted to hear about them again. From her.

This wasn't just a threat. It was an actual attempt to follow through on the threat.

"I had two visits on Monday that required police escorts," she said, her voice steady, her gaze clear and professional as she sat down in her chair and faced the detective. "One is a convicted felon, out on probation after serving three years for felonious assault. James Barber. He's living with a woman he met while he was in prison and she's got a four-year-old. I'm there be-cause of a report from a grandmother who wants the child removed from the home."

Riley stiffened. It was the first he'd heard of that.

Because he'd chosen to leave and make his own report the night before, rather than staying while she spoke with the officer.

He'd just found out about their baby, and he'd run away again.

She was going to figure out right quick that it was what he did. As soon as he'd turned eighteen, he'd moved out of the house. And when he'd graduated from Quantico, he'd quit going home for family dinners.

When Brody had needed a place to stay during his college breaks, he'd failed to offer one of the two empty bedrooms in the old house he'd bought with an eye to fixing it up...

"The second is two women, the Thompsons, both

ex-cons, both who served time for domestic violence. They hooked up in prison. Both have been out a while, been married a couple of years, but there's obvious violence going on in the home. Charges were brought against both of them recently for disturbing the peace. Their fights are violent and loud enough that neighbors call the police, but neither of them will admit to hurting the other, and neither will press charges. They were fined for disturbing the peace, but having me visit once a week, in an attempt to help them learn healthy ways to love each other and live together, and to keep an eye on the home, was part of their sentence. Neither of them wants me there and because of that, and because of their obvious violent tendencies, I'm not to visit without an escort."

Riley listened, impressed and uncomfortable at the same time. She was pregnant. Carrying their child. He didn't want her walking into the home of two known violent offenders...

"You said you thought the driver last night was male, right?" Iglesias was looking at Riley.

"I couldn't be sure, but I thought so, yes. I'm certain the shooter today was." His brain kicked into full fight mode. "Obviously, we're looking at the same perp. Unless there are two small older black pickup trucks owned by two different people who don't like Charlize."

Iglesias nodded. "And I'd say the Thompsons are out," he said, "though I'm still going to pay them a visit. But the fact that the guy missed this morning... if he was a hired gun he likely wouldn't have done so. He was one man, not two women, and he missed, so it's not likely he was someone hired by the two women."

Sadie's pick grew even higher in Riley's estimation as the man stated what Riley had already been thinking.

"And...there's one more that stands out," Charlize said, her gaze completely on the detective. She hadn't looked at Riley since they'd all sat back down. "Mostly because of a phone call I had this morning."

She hadn't mentioned this to him. Riley felt slighted. Had to adjust his thinking to get rid of the unwarranted reaction. And listened intently as the mother of his future child relayed the conversation to the detective, including the fact that a potential abuser's girlfriend was scared and wanted her off the case. Ronny Simms and his girlfriend, Laurene Dill. New names on Riley's radar. Though he trusted Iglesias to do his job, Riley was already on his cell phone. Typing in the guy's full name. Looking at the photo that came up. A mug shot.

"Is this him?" he asked, holding the phone out to her.

She nodded. "But he's never actually done any physical violence that I'm aware of," she said, being fair, just as he'd expect her to be.

"Is that the guy you saw behind the wheel?" Iglesias asked Riley, and as much as Riley wanted to be sure it was, he wasn't sure.

Looking at the phone again, he shook his head. "He's white and has dark hair," he said, "but there's nothing about this guy here that strikes me as familiar."

He hadn't been looking at the guy's face as he might have done any other time he'd been witness to a potential crime. As he should have been doing.

Instead, both times, the majority of his attention had been on the victim. Even before the attempts on her life had happened.

He hadn't been watching his surroundings at all times as he'd been trained to do. He'd been watching her.

"I'd like you to stay inside, at least until I can check some of this out," Iglesias said, his expression forthright and serious as he looked her in the eye. Charlize nodded, wanting to trust the detective completely. She wanted to look at Riley, too, make certain that he was in agreement, but wouldn't let herself.

"I've already rearranged my visits for the day, and the rest I can do from home," she said. "And what about my aunt? Should I call her home?"

The man shook his head. "It's clear this guy is after you. I'll put an officer on your house, and, when your aunt's ready to come home, she should have an escort. Just until I dig a little deeper here. If we have reason to suspect any of these names you've given me, we can put a man on them. It could turn out to be someone else in your case files, too," he added. "Or something completely unconnected…"

Too many *if*s for her. "What's your professional opinion?" she asked. She worked with the police department regularly. Was privy to a lot of inside scoop.

"That it's going to turn out to be Ronny or James," he said. "But I'm not willing to bet your life on that."

She glanced at Riley then. She hadn't meant to but…

"There's something else you should know, Detective. But something I need to ask you to keep to yourself as much as possible as no one else in my life knows yet…"

Riley's entire body stiffened, his face deadpan. But

he didn't in any way indicate that she should keep her mouth shut.

"I'm pregnant," she said, feeling the words to her core as she heard them announced to a near stranger.

It wasn't just a nightmare. A dread. A fantasy. A hope.

Her pregnancy was real.

And if her life was in danger, her baby's could be, too.

"Does the father know?"

She specifically did not look at Riley as she nodded.

"Did he know before yesterday's threat?"

She shook her head.

"But he knew before this morning's phone call?"

She got where Iglesias was going with his questioning, and knew, of course, that he was all wrong. But she couldn't out Riley. Not until they'd at least talked about it and he had a chance to speak with his family.

It was the decent thing to do.

"He did. But he's not angry about it," she said, realizing that she spoke the complete truth. And that Riley's lack of anger mattered. A lot. Meant a lot.

Not that he had a right to be mad at her—the condom had been his—but he could be angry at its failure. At fate.

And he hadn't expressed even a hint of that.

He wasn't happy she was pregnant. But he wasn't upset, either...

"I think the pregnancy is pertinent in terms of anyone watching out for Charlize, but it doesn't seem to be an issue in terms of what we're looking at here," Riley was saying. "Obviously, since no one else in her life knows yet, her clients couldn't know or have some reason to take exception to her because of it, nor would anyone else who might be making these threats and attempts against her life."

He was right, too. She just knew that when you talked to the police, they expected you to tell them everything important in your life, just in case. And she'd needed anyone who might come upon her injured to know that she had a baby's life to save, in addition to her own.

Not that she was planning to be injured. She wasn't. "I've been trained both in self-defense and in self-protection," she announced to the room in general.

"It might not even be an issue after today," Detective Iglesias said. "If the perp's one of our guys here—" he nodded toward the notebook he'd been jotting in "—and if we can match a vehicle to him, or match either him or the vehicle to any surveillance cameras that might be in the area, we could have this wrapped up pretty quickly."

She liked the sound of that. Liked it a whole lot. Glanced at Riley as the detective's phone rang and he excused himself to take the call. Riley was watching her, his expression kind of odd. Like a concerned friend or something.

Not professional. Not like a lover or enemy, either. But like he honestly just cared about her well-being.

She'd have taken the idea for granted during the night she'd known him. It made no sense coming from the man who'd walked out on her after leading her on all night. He'd gotten the sex he'd obviously been after. And there'd been nothing left there of any interest to him.

Not even enough affection to warrant an "I'll call

you." Or enough friendship to have called to tell her that he'd enjoyed getting to know her—just because making such a call was a decent thing to do.

Riley Colton had had ample opportunity and he didn't do the decent thing. But had her pregnancy changed things? she wondered.

That fact had to remain in the forefront of her mind, and as a barrier to her heart, as they figured out how to disarm the land mine upon which they were sitting.

Breaking eye contact with Charlize, Riley stood, walked toward the window, paying attention to the surroundings as he waited for Iglesias to finish his call. Close attention. He had to get on with business. Focus on the case. Get his ass out of Charlize's presence and figure out what he was going to do about the baby she was carrying.

How he was going to tell his family, for one.

Because clearly he was going to have to. It wasn't like Charlize was going to keep it a secret. Or even be able to do so once she started showing.

He wondered how her aunt was going to take the news. Figured that Blythe might be shocked—but overall, loving and supportive.

A good thing. A relief, really, to know that she'd have familial support.

He dreaded telling his.

Had no idea what he was going to tell them.

He knew his sisters way too well to think that he could just drop the news and move on. No, they'd have a million questions apiece. From holding him accountable, to asking if they could help name the baby. At least two of them were going to want immediate roles.

Vikki would just decide her role and proceed accordingly. Sadie, he wasn't sure about. As caught up as she was with Tate, their wedding and plans for their future together, she might not take as active an interest…

Business. The case.

Iglesias ended his call. "About this RevitaYou thing…" he started.

Turning from the window, Riley stood there, looking directly at the detective, but watching Charlize peripherally. "Charlize is involved there, too," Riley said. He'd intimated as much when he'd called the detective to move their morning appointment to Charlize's town home. He explained the basics of the scheme, as he knew them, telling Iglesias about Brody's connection to his family and the state the younger man had been in when he'd come begging for help the day before. He then added, "Charlize's aunt, who lives here with her, is an investor in that last group with Brody. She's out fifty thousand, as well. The only difference is, she put up her life savings, rather than borrowing the money like Brody did. I'm assuming, since Matthews put Brody onto to Capital X, he also sent others their way. And if, like Brody, they're in that last group, they're going to be facing the same kind of pressure he is."

Iglesias asked about Capital X, and Riley told him what he knew from his time at the FBI, and added that Griffin had a contact and was looking into them.

"Ironic that your life is threatened—" the detective looked at Charlize, and then toward Riley "—at the same time your brother is threatened and comes to you for help," he said.

Riley nodded, had already gone down that road. "I don't think there's a connection," he said. "There's no way anyone would have known that I was on my way to see Blythe Kent, certainly not in enough time to get to the house…"

"And the warning was clearly for me yesterday, not for Riley." She glanced at him fully, and they were on the same side again, working together. He much preferred it that way.

"Exactly. I was on the same sidewalk. Another few yards down and he could have delivered the warning to me. I'm the one who's investigating. The one Brody came to. If this had anything to do with RevitaYou, with Brody, why warn Charlize and then shoot at her today?"

"Are you sure the guy wasn't shooting at you?" Iglesias asked, but seemed to just be making sure they were looking at every angle.

Riley nodded. "I hadn't stepped outside yet."

"Okay—" the detective nodded toward Riley "—then I'd say the perp picked a bad time to come after Charlize, or fate was watching out for you," he said, glancing at Charlize, "in having him heading your way to talk to your aunt when he did…

"I've seen it happen that way more often than I can dismiss," Iglesias continued.

Riley wasn't into philosophizing. Never had been.

"I don't understand why, with almost a million dollars gone, more of these investors haven't come forward," he said, needing to get the conversation firmly back on track before his life started to derail completely. There was no way fate was bringing him and Charlize back together. It was coincidence. Every bit of it.

And he didn't even want to know what she was making of the detective's statements. Probably dismissing them, just like him.

"I did some checking after you called last night," Iglesias was saying. "Turns out there were sixteen separate police complaints about a banker named Wes Matthews. Nothing concrete, just reports that people feel they've been conned since they can't reach the guy. He seems to have vanished, along with the RevitaYou site. I've started an official file and will be handling the case."

Riley filled him in on the mysterious scientist who also seemed to be missing. He also gave the detective a rundown of the work assigned to his siblings and employees, letting Iglesias know that he'd keep him fully apprised as soon as he knew anything.

It wasn't uncommon for the GRPD to work with professional investigation firms—and Iglesias expressed his appreciation to Riley and Colton PI, agreeing to fully reciprocate the sharing of information.

And then, with one more warning to Charlize to stay inside and watch her back, saying again that he'd have an officer on the house within an hour, the detective was gone.

Taking with him the protection from any possibility of personal conversation between Riley and Charlize.

"I'm staying until the officer gets here," he said.

Her nod didn't surprise him. She was a reasonable person.

"And we need to talk," he added.

If Iglesias was any good at his job, he was going to be telling whatever officer was assigned to Charlize's house that she was pregnant. And his siblings all had contacts with the GRPD. No telling whether the trail could lead them to hearing the news from someone other than him, not that he'd been outed as the father yet.

She nodded again. Sat down on the couch, kicking off her sandals and crossing her legs. Looking far too young for him. And far too sexy for him not to notice her in spite of their age difference—kind of a moot point when you considered that he'd already impregnated her.

But what you did for a night was far different than what you'd do for a lifetime. Or even should do.

"So talk," she said.

Riley opened his mouth to speak. Needing to make things right.

And no words came out.

Chapter 8

If Charlize had been at her best, she'd have helped him. As it was, she sat there on her couch, watching Riley Colton wrestle for words, and...just let him struggle.

She was a certified family counselor. She not only knew healthy interpersonal dynamics, but also knew how to teach them to those in unhealthy patterns. There were no lessons in her books that fit the man who'd walked from the window toward her, and back again several times—showing her a perfect male backside displayed deliciously in the tight black jeans on one side, and when he turned, the thick mass of upper arm muscle defined by the short sleeves of his polo shirt. She wouldn't look at his chest. Or his fly.

Both held way too many memories of the night she'd spent in fantasyland with him. She couldn't afford to burn again.

If he continued to silently pace, the officer would be there and Riley'd have no excuse to prolong what had to be agony for him. The silence between them was starting to feel like it to her, too.

She could let him off the hook. Tell him she neither expected nor wanted anything from him. The sentiments were true. She'd known from the first missed period that if she was pregnant she was going to have the baby and raise it on her own.

She wasn't going to settle as her mother had, time and time again.

Eventually, he sat on the chair she'd occupied earlier, perched on the front half of it, legs spread, elbows on his knees. He could have been relaxed. But looked more ready to spring up and out the front door at the sound of a buzzer.

"I've gone the whole relationship route…doesn't work for me. But I expect full rights as a father."

Whatever she'd been expecting, that was not it. Hugging her knees to her chest, she closed herself off to him. He was not going to…

What?

She had to find out… "What do you consider full rights?"

"Financially, I'll pay support, of course."

She'd been prepared to accept that he might do that. The money could go in a college fund. She didn't share any of her thoughts, though. Just waited.

"And…we'll need to set up some kind of visitation schedule. It's not ideal. I'm not saying overnight. Personally, I'd rather my child sleep every night in the same home, though I have no grounds for thinking that would be best…"

She frowned, her stomach clenched so tight she was afraid she might start to feel sick again. Almost wished on the malady so she could escape the room. The conversation. "So you want the child to spend all nights at your place? Or no nights?" It was all just hypothetical. She didn't have to agree. He could take her to court.

He didn't even want to be a father. He'd said so. Quite clearly.

"The child should have time with me."

Not that *he* wanted the time. But the child should have it. He apparently had given up on the night idea. As though the baby just wouldn't sleep.

Almost fascinated now, she continued to let him squirm in his own juices.

"My sisters are going to be up in your space instantly. I have no control over them whatsoever, and once they know there's going to be a baby in the family…well… I'm just letting you know…fair warning…"

She nodded. If they got out of hand, that was what restraining orders were for. If not, she'd love for her baby to have a big, welcoming family. To feel wanted and loved. To have someone to run to when Charlize pissed him or her off, as surely she would, just as Charlize herself had run to Blythe when she'd thought her grandparents were being too strict.

He stood. Moved to the window. "A police car just pulled up," he said, sounding as though he'd just lost a hundred pounds off his back. "That's it, then. I'm going to call a meeting with my siblings this afternoon—for as soon as they can all get there—and I'll check in with you after that."

He was heading toward the door. "And I'll call you if I hear from Iglesias."

Still sitting on the couch, nonplussed and she didn't know what else, Charlize watched him stop in the archway leading to the foyer and the front door. She wasn't following him.

Didn't think their conversation was anywhere near over.

But she understood that the business awaiting him was far more urgent than their baby's visitation schedule. If there'd be one. And they were going to be interrupted again any second.

"I'd appreciate it if you keep me apprised...even if it's just a text..."

"Apprised of what?" She was being purposefully difficult. She knew it. But couldn't stop herself. The man got under her skin.

"Anything. Everything. If you feel sick. If anyone shows up here uninvited, if there's any more trouble... including troublesome phone calls..."

"I'll call the police."

"For morning sickness?" Riley asked.

Ahhh. So he wasn't as lost as she'd thought.

"I'm not going to text you every time I get sick."

A knock sounded on the door.

"Just keep me apprised," he said then, grabbing her gaze with his own and compelling her to not look away. "Please."

At that, she nodded. He'd asked nicely.

And, past experience had shown her, giving him what he wanted was a sure way to get rid of him.

And she needed him to go. Even if part of her wanted him to stay.

* * *

Riley didn't like leaving Charlize, but after satisfying himself that the officer who'd arrived would keep a diligent watch on her, he was eager to get back to doing what he did best. Finding the bad guys and taking them down.

Other guys were good at spending quality time with the family.

His life purpose was making the world a safer place for the families to spend their quality time.

And now, more than ever, with a child of his own soon to be needing a safe place to grow up, he was determined to get out on the streets and rid them of every piece of dirt he saw.

After a call from Ashanti, he went to work on another of his cases: the disappearance of Shannon Martin. He headed to a warehouse where a woman who'd once danced with Shannon Martin managed a plant that made leather jazz shoes. Those kind of shoes a serious dancer wore, Ashanti had told him, as opposed to the more cheaply made versions worn by a lot of young girls and hobbyist dancers. There were only a few places in the United States that actually manufactured the shoes—a brand worn by Shannon—and one of them was right there in Grand Rapids. Since Shannon had been at a rehearsal the day she'd disappeared, he was interested in speaking with the former dancer. She was someone the police had never interviewed.

And twenty minutes after entering the managing office at the shoe factory, he was leaving with renewed energy. With adrenaline flowing with good force. With a reminder that he did what he did because he had a sense for knowing where to sniff.

The witness recalled Shannon Martin had seen a father abusing his young daughter in a deserted dressing room backstage.

The shoe manager couldn't remember the young dancer's name, but she knew the father's because the guy had given her and Shannon the creeps. The incident had taken place more than a year before Shannon's disappearance so the show manager hadn't thought anything of it.

When Riley had heard the guy's name, recognized it from a case he'd worked years before, he thought enough of the information to call Ashanti and have her do some more research.

They likely weren't going to end up with good news for Avis, but he had a feeling Avis was prepared for that eventuality. The man had already grieved for the loss of his sister. What he needed was answers.

He needed them, too. For Brody. And, as immediately, for the woman carrying Riley's unborn child. Because he had no idea where Brody was, and had to hope the young man's street smarts were keeping him somewhat protected, he went, first to do his own drive-bys of Charlize's clients' names and expected whereabouts he'd committed to memory that morning. Both of the Thompson women were at their jobs. James Barber was at his. And Ronny Simms was accounted for, too. He didn't speak with any of the suspects. But once he was satisfied that none of them were on their way to Charlize's place, he was able to get his focus back on RevitaYou, Wes Matthews and finding the thugs from Capital X before they found Brody and began breaking more bones.

On his way back to CI headquarters, he called Charlize, just to make sure that, since he hadn't heard anything, she was fine. She barely had a second to speak to him, having put someone on hold to answer his call, had said she was working. When he told her that the three top suspects in the threats on her were currently occupied, she thanked him. And hung up before he could ask how she was feeling—if her morning sickness was carrying on into the day.

Pal met him at the kitchen door as he walked in from the back entrance. Wagging her tail, she waited for his pat on the head, but in so doing, told him that everything at the house was okay. Bailey came into the kitchen to meet him.

"I've been to every one of the Grand Rapids sites where RevitaYou seminars were held," he said, following Riley through to his office as he spoke. "Wes Matthews dealt with them directly. From what I can tell there was no middle person, no secretary. He handled all of the details and paid cash. The contact number they had for him was the same one Brody had. I can't find anything on the scientist."

"Put Ashanti on him...see if..."

"Already done. I caught her before she left," the tall, dark young man interrupted. "So far nothing connects Matthews to any scientist."

"A couple of site managers I talked to had spoken to some of the people who gave testimonials. Both of them said they believe the testimonials were completely true. The people were just normal. One of them even knew one of the first investors, knew firsthand that she'd made money reselling the product, which was why she let them use her facility for a seminar. The facilities manager also said she's been taking RevitaYou and has had good results." Bailey gave Riley names and addresses, which he jotted down to relay to his siblings in their upcoming meetings.

"And I spoke with several of the investors themselves. And, through them, talked to some of the RevitaYou users they'd personally sold to." He frowned, came forward and stood in front of Riley's desk. "Some of them had no problems, but half said that they felt nauseated after taking them, Riley. Just like Brody's girlfriend. For a couple, it was worse than just nausea. One woman I saw isn't doing well at all. Her doctor's running tests, but since they know she's ingested something new recently, they're wondering if she's been poisoned."

The news pissed Riley off. In the way he got pissed at injustice. It was just a thing with him—this inability to let wrongdoing slide off his back.

"I've only spoken with half a dozen users so far," Bailey was saying, "so the results could be skewed, but when Ashanti said you were on your way back, I stopped in to let you know, and write up notes. This sounds like some messed up stuff…"

Riley took the notes Bailey handed him and thanked the younger man. He heard the back door open and close, followed by Pippa's greeting to Pal in the baby voice she sometimes used with the dog, so went in to get snacks on the dining room table for the upcoming meeting. As busy as everyone was, he had to make certain they had enough food to keep their minds as sharp as possible.

If he timed it just right, maybe he could get the personal news he had to tell them out while all five of their mouths were full. Giving them all a couple of chewing seconds to think before just blurting out what first came to their minds—the judgment and doubts that he could do without.

Business was first and as soon as they'd all taken their seats, he started right in, filling them all in on his meeting with Emmanuel Iglesias, thanking Sadie for the referral.

"I've assured him that we'll keep him apprised of anything we find out, and he's agreed to return the favor," he told the group, pausing only long enough to see a nod from everyone. Maintaining Colton Investigations' good relationship with law enforcement was something he took very seriously.

"I've tried repeatedly to text both numbers we have for Brody, and got nothing," he added. All four girls chimed in that they'd tried, too, but no one had heard from him. Griffin remained silent, not surprising to Riley. The adoption attorney was on board, but he evidently wasn't losing as much sleep over Brody's disappearance as the rest of them were.

When he looked up and caught Riley looking at him, he said, "Brody's always been one to look for a quick fix but he's also scary smart." He looked at his sisters as he spoke. "And he's still got those street smarts in him. He needs us to get him out of this mess, but in the meantime he'll find a way to keep himself safe until *we* fix the big issue."

While Riley found Griffin's attempt to reassure their sisters a bit on the rough side, he also agreed with the gist of what he'd said.

And reported on Bailey's findings before starting around the table for their reports. Feeling like a stopwatch, clicking down the time to his own doom. He had to tell them. Who knew how many officers would be involved in the protection detail outside of Charlize's house? Not that her pregnancy would be connected personally to him...

"I was able to get a hold of the surveillance footage from Brody's office building, only the lobby and just outside," Pippa said. "I've been over it several times, and have sent it to Ashanti to see if there's anything she can pull out that I didn't see," she said, her expression as serious as her demeanor generally was. Pippa was most like Riley in some ways—all about work. "I see Brody coming off the elevator, looking around. I see him head toward the door. Then on the outside footage, I see him come through the door to the outside. I can even see him seem to notice someone, and then speak, but whoever he's talking to stayed just beyond reach of the camera. There's a pillar on each side of the building. Brody walks off screen and then...nothing. He never comes back through those doors for the rest of the day."

"Pip sent me the video, just in case, and I pulled out every visible person and ran them all through facial recognition. Nothing popped," Sadie added.

"Unfortunately, this validates the theory that the Capital X thugs are professional enforcers," Vikki said. "They knew how not to be seen, while still intimidating him. Avoiding waiting for him in the lobby, out of reach of all cameras, and yet, right there on the front steps where everyone who works with Brody passes by."

"I was able to connect with a couple of people who've used Capital X in the past," Griffin said. "With the assurance that their names won't be made public, of course." Everyone nodded again, all focus on their adopted brother. "Both sources gave me the same information. They seem to have unlimited resources, as there's no limit to the amount of money you can take out in a loan and their interest rates are very high, thirty percent. They operate solely underground. No one knows of any office space or physical presence of any kind of business front. And digitally it's all on the dark web. No one knows the name of their kingpin. Everyone deals with an anonymous contact at Capital X and the only way to communicate telephonically is with burner phones. Both of my sources paid off the loans as agreed, but both intimated that they'd been told what would happen if they didn't. These guys don't take people's homes from them—they break their bodies, just like Brody said."

Riley noticed a couple of winces on either side of him, and figured everyone was thinking about Brody's two broken fingers that Riley had told them about.

"I asked around about Capital X," Vikki inserted then, her long blond hair perfectly styled, as usual. "No one knows who's behind the name, but they have a very clear reputation just the same. From what I heard, their unlimited capital comes from their despicable tactics combined with the hellacious interest rates. They prey on the neediest and most desperate. You know, if you have means to pay back a loan, an accredited bank will give you the money. And if you don't, there's Capital X, ready and willing to take full advantage."

Everything he was hearing gelled with what Riley had ascertained during his time at the FBI. Capital X was only a name, covering for a phantom boss that was the devil incarnate.

Now that he was independently employed, no longer having to work only the cases he was assigned by the higher-ups, he was going to find this bastard and take him down.

Period.

"Brody said Wes Matthews referred him to Capital X," he said, noting that not one of his siblings had taken a bite of the bagged, precut apple slices he'd dropped into a bowl. They hadn't touched the cashews, either. "Maybe we can find a connection from Matthews that will lead us to the loan shark."

"I checked into Wes Matthews." Kiely brushed at her bangs as she spoke. "The man's banking record is clean. At least on the surface. It looks like this is his first foray into the pyramid scheme world."

"Which would explain why we haven't heard anything about it, why it hasn't been in the media," Riley interjected.

"Since he's newly criminal, we can hope that he'll make missteps and be more easily found," Griffin offered, taking an apple slice.

Finally. They had to eat. He needed full mouths so he could make his announcement, bring the meeting to an end and get everyone out there working hard to get Brody safely home.

"I spoke with the investor whose card Brody had," he said then. "The one I told you about this morning. Her name's Blythe Kent. She's in her late seventies, and while she had some great things to say about Brody, about how kind he was to her the day they'd both attended the seminar, she only had a couple of other pieces of information that might help. She's been taking the vitamins herself and has been feeling a bit nauseated. I think we need to seriously think about alerting the public about these things."

"From what you said Bailey relayed, I agree with you," Sadie said, and the others nodded.

"I'll give Iglesias a call and see if he can get an official press release out from the GRPD," Riley told them.

"Ms. Kent also said that the scientist who created the vitamins was at the seminar. Brody hadn't mentioned it, but she said he gave an in-depth slide show talking about the different compounds he used and how they work together to make healthy skin cells. She couldn't remember the guy's name."

"I'll look into him," Sadie said.

"If we weren't already fully on this case for Brody's sake, we'd have taken it on for Ms. Kent," Riley added. "She's been swindled out of fifty grand of her life's savings."

"So who's going to look for a connection between Matthews and Capital X?" Vikki asked.

Griffin and Kiely both volunteered.

"Okay," Riley said. "Both of you, work together on it."

Vikki and Sadie reached for the cashews at the same time. Pippa took an apple. Kiely was busy talking in an aside to Griffin. The meeting was breaking up. They all had places to be and weren't going to hang around just because he wasn't ready to drop his bomb on the table.

For a second there, Riley considered putting it off. Wondered what his chances were of being able to permanently avoid the topic.

Guys had kids their families didn't know about.

It happened.

But not to the Coltons.

His parents had taught him, and he'd helped them

teach the rest… Coltons were always honest with each other.

There was no way he was getting out of this.

And while his siblings gathered their things, he prayed for an escape route, anyway.

Chapter 9

Sadie stood up.

"I need to speak with you all about something else," Riley blurted, somewhat awkwardly. Suddenly, the only sound in the room was Pal's panting. All sets of green eyes, and one hazel, pointed straight at him. Sadie dropped back to her chair.

And no one chewed.

Damn.

Those eyes working together as an excruciating spotlight, Riley cleared his throat. Reached for an apple. Something innocuous. Normal. Took a bite, letting it fill his suddenly dry mouth with juice.

"What's going on?"

"What's wrong?"

"What's up?"

"Talk."

"Is everything okay?"

Kiely, Pippa, Griffin, Vikki and Sadie. All talking at once, but he heard them in order. As he always did. Years of law enforcement training did that for a guy.

"I recognized Blythe Kent's name when her card fell out of Brody's brochures. Which is why I chose to be the one to follow up with her."

"Was she a friend of Mom's?" Pippa asked.

He shook his head. "I'd never met Blythe. I know her niece, who lives with her."

A couple of blond heads cocked one way. Brown another. And Griffin got a bit of a grin as he faced Riley head-on.

"You like her!" Sadie exclaimed.

About to say he'd only met her once, Riley checked himself. His siblings needed to know about the baby. They didn't need to know that the child was a result of a one-night stand.

That story didn't really feel like his to tell.

Trouble was, he didn't have any story to tell. Any words at all. No explanation that suited him or the situation.

"She's pregnant." The baldness of the words left a bad sound in his head. And came to him partially in Charlize's voice, talking to Iglesias that morning.

"The child is mine."

Damn, again.

After another second or two of dropped jaws and opened mouths, the room erupted. So much so that Pal barked.

And Riley did something he'd never done to them before. He got up and walked out.

* * *

When her phone rang late that day, Charlize expected the caller to be Riley. Wasn't happy about the initial disappointment that briefly swept through her as she saw Detective Iglesias's ID come up on her screen.

Nor was she happy about the wave of anxiety the detective's name brought. Considered letting the call go to voice mail.

She was a strong, trained and capable woman. No way some creep was going to make her live in fear.

Or scare her off her job, either.

But she had an added, unexpected challenge, too. A baby to protect. A random thought of raising a child all on her own brought another short wave of panic.

She pushed back at it.

She was just going to have to figure out how to do it all.

Had tried on and off all afternoon to come up with a scenario that had her accomplishing everything successfully—while she actually did complete the work she'd set for herself to do from home. Reports were written and written well. Calls had been made. A woman she'd been working with had finally agreed to enter rehab and she'd made those arrangements.

She picked up on the fifth ring. You didn't take control by avoidance...

"I wish I had something more to tell you than I do," the detective started out. "I spoke with everyone on your client list, those you saw Monday, and otherwise, and every one of them have alibis for yesterday's drive-by threat, and this morning's shooting. Including James Barber and Ronny Simms. Everyone is at work today, too, on time, as expected."

"Ronny and James both had alibis?" she asked. She'd been telling herself the threat would be gone by the end of the day. Neither James nor Ronny were hard-core thugs, or even all that bright. They had anger issues, jealousy issues, but they'd made mistakes. Neither of them was good at covering their tracks, which was how they'd ended up on police radar, and then in court and on her client list, to begin with.

"Last night's alibis for both Barber and Simms, and one other, as well, were given by their girlfriends, but yes, all three women looked me in the eye and told me their boyfriends were with them. And you're sure that there was no one else in the truck last night?"

"I'm not sure, no," she said, getting up from the desk in her upstairs office and pacing to the window, before deciding that that wasn't safe. She could be shot through a window. Still, it had been good to see the police car stationed out front. It would be a deterrent if nothing else, right? "I didn't see much of the driver. Riley Colton did, though."

"I have him on my list to call next," Iglesias said. "And even if no one saw a second occupant of the truck, someone could have ducked down on the seat or the floor."

"What about the black truck?"

"No one on your client list claimed it, and there isn't one registered to any of them."

"Riley said the truck that sped away this morning didn't have a plate on it, so that would mean it's probably not registered, right?"

"Or that the plates were removed so that the truck couldn't be identified."

Either way, that left her with nothing but threats and suspicions.

And fear.

"I'm going to be keeping an officer on your house for tonight, and we'll reassess tomorrow," he said.

She worked with the court system, and with the police. She knew what he was telling her. They weren't going to have the manpower to continue to watch her twenty-four-seven.

She really had thought it would all just be over.

"We've also alerted everyone on the street to keep eyes on Barber, Simms and a couple of others," he added. "If anyone heads your way, we'll know, and we'll stop them."

In a perfect world. They'd try, though. She trusted that completely. "Thank you," she told him, truly appreciative of all that he was doing for her.

"Take good care," he told her and hung up, leaving her with a helpless feeling that she was determined would not win.

The threat had to be coming from one of her clients. She was the clear target—not her aunt, not Riley, not anyone else. She'd been told to stay away—before she'd even known about Aunt Blythe's involvement with Wes Matthews and RevitaYou.

And the only thing in her life that anyone would have any cause to want her gone from was a case. An unhealthy home whose occupants were feeling threatened by her presence in their lives.

But if she let them scare her off, she'd be giving a dangerous person more power.

Power that they would likely use to hurt or kill a mate.

She couldn't live with that on her conscience. Or her heart.

She couldn't let evil win.

Riley hadn't just walked out of the meeting in his dining room. He'd walked out of his house. Without keys. He had a gun at his waist. A wallet in his pocket. But no keys.

For the first minute or two, he just strode at a good clip, heading nowhere in particular except away. He wasn't running away. He'd go back. He'd face them. Maybe not within the next hour, or even that night, but he'd stand up to whatever trial his siblings wanted to put him on.

As soon as he figured out the answers to the questions they were all bound to have.

Answers they would expect from him.

Answers they deserved.

After a few minutes of calming exercise, he slowed his pace a bit. And knew where he was headed. It was only a few blocks between his place and Charlize's, in the upscale, historical Heritage Park neighborhood he'd grown up in and had thought he'd left forever.

Life had a way of turning on a dime. His almost half century of living had damn sure shown him that.

Charlize didn't have to know he was there. He'd feel better just seeing the cop outside in a quiet, undisturbed neighborhood.

A little better, anyway. The woman was clearly in danger.

Which meant his child was in danger.

While he did nothing but wait for others to figure it out. And to watch over her.

The idea wasn't sitting well with him. To the point that he knew the plan wasn't going to work. He'd given his entire adult life to protecting and serving. No way in hell he wasn't going to do the same for his own flesh and blood.

This strong inner conversation was interrupted by the ring of his cell phone. Grabbing it out of his pocket, he listened intently, and without pleasure, to the report Iglesias gave him.

Basically, they were nowhere with nothing.

Unacceptable.

Thanking the detective, certain that the man was going to continue to keep diligent watch on Charlize's clients, Riley stood just down from Charlize's house. He leaned against a tree by the curb as he filled Iglesias in on the meeting at CI that afternoon.

"My team has connected with six RevitaYou users, and three of them complained of not feeling well," he reported. "Blythe Kent reported feelings of nausea, as well. I'm thinking there needs to be some formal looking into those vitamins. We might have more than a pyramid scheme on our hands..."

"I'll talk to the chief about it," Iglesias told him, and agreeing, once again, to keep each other informed, they rang off.

Iglesias was a good guy. And in some ways, his hands were tied.

Riley's weren't anymore. A definite upside to being an independent professional investigator. He could spend what time he chose on whatever case he chose. Look into whatever he chose to look into.

He could offer his services as he pleased, or thought warranted.

And at the moment he had one place in mind to plant his ass.

The idea was just starting to form on a conscious level and yet it was concrete. Charlize and her aunt had to come stay with him at CI headquarters.

And it would all go so much better if she was agreeable with the plan.

Stopping at the cop car out front, he introduced himself, showed his professional investigator ID and then headed toward Charlize's front door.

He should probably call first. Had the thought. Dismissed it. Time was of the essence.

And he wasn't going to rest until he knew she was safe.

Charlize had just hung up from calling her aunt at the neighbor's when the knock sounded on the door. Heart pounding, she kept out of sight of the front window, half hugging the wall as she made her way to the foyer and the peephole in the front door. Could just be the police officer out front, but if he was knocking on the door, it might not be good.

As soon as she recognized Riley Colton standing on her stoop, she unlocked and pulled open the door, keeping herself behind it and out of sight from the street as he let himself inside.

She wasn't sure what they had to say to each other. What had to be said right then, at any rate, but she wasn't going to stand in the open doorway and speak to him.

"Iglesias called," she told him, straight off. He'd been present during both attempts on her life, he was the father of her child and a career FBI man. She could do the math. There was no way he was going to mind his own business on this one.

She wasn't even sure she wanted him to do so. The man knew how to face danger and win. If he had advice for her, she wanted to hear it.

"I spoke with him, as well," Riley said, standing there in those tight jeans with that gun on his belt, looking all masculine and sexy. "Which is why I'm here."

Of course. He wouldn't be stopping by just to see her.

Not that she wanted him to stop by just to see her. She'd send him away if he did.

"My aunt is calling her sister, my aunt Grace, who lives out in Lowell, to see about staying with her until this all blows over," she blurted, lest he get any idea she couldn't take care of her family.

Aunt Blythe didn't know about the baby yet and she'd decided to keep that piece of information to herself for the moment.

The older woman had already been upset about having been scammed, and Charlize had had to tell her about the threats on her life. She couldn't have Blythe walking around a danger zone without knowing to take care. Couldn't risk having her caught in any crossfire.

"I'll be driving her out there shortly," she continued. Lowell was built on both sides of the Flat River, encompassing three city miles with a population of just over four thousand people. Its Main Street was still a place Aunt Blythe and Aunt Grace could safely walk down to have dinner at the local diner. Aunt Grace had lived in the small town for decades, ever since she'd married, and Charlize had many happy memories of visiting the town and attending the famous showboat entertainment that used to run every summer…

"I'll go with you," Riley said, interrupting her attempt to get lost in minutiae that felt good—that built up her somewhat depleted sense of control. "And then I want you to come stay with me," he added, so completely serious and calm, she almost thought she'd misunderstood him.

"What?" She frowned at him. Shook her head. Took a step backward.

Things were just careening too far out of control. She couldn't find any normal—no matter where she looked.

"You shouldn't be here alone. CI Headquarters has plenty of room—we had eight of us living there once and managed to get along—and I'm armed and trained. Pal's there. And I can't not protect my child. And the woman carrying it. Period. You can ask me to not do so, tell me to not do so, order me to go away and not come back, and I'll be back, even if it means you filing a restraining order against me…"

Taken aback, but not completely in a negative way, Charlize stared at him. He was half acting like a macho alpha male, and half begging. The combination didn't compute, and yet there she was, witnessing it.

"I'm hoping you aren't going to put me through any further distress than we're already facing, by arguing the point and bringing said restraining order into reality," he said then, his tone more like himself. Logical. Calm. Controlled.

"Who's Pal?" She needed time.

Had to think. Something she was finding increasingly difficult anytime Riley Colton was around.

Which was one good solid reason why she couldn't stay with him. Couldn't do as he'd asked.

There were others, too. They'd come to her as soon as she could think.

"My German shepherd. She's a trained watch dog, but unless there's danger around, she tends to forget that. She also doubles pretty well as a vacuum cleaner and floor mop when food's involved."

The tough guy had a dog. A dog he clearly adored.

"I've told my siblings about you, so if you're worried about what they'd think, you staying there, there's no need."

Falling back against the wall, she leaned. "You told them what about me?"

"That your aunt was scammed by RevitaYou, and that you're pregnant with my baby."

"You told them that."

"I had to. You told Iglesias."

He'd mentioned something about it earlier, about his sisters being aunts...and there'd be an uncle in the mix, too.

It was all happening too fast.

Which was partially on her. She'd suspected the pregnancy for weeks. Had kept the possibility to herself.

"I *had* to tell Iglesias. My life is in danger. They had to know that there's a baby whose life could also be in danger..."

As soon as she said the words, even before she saw his eyes darken, she knew she'd just walked herself right into his plan.

"Did you tell them about the one-night stand, too?" How humiliating. And...stupid.

"Of course not."

There was no *of course* about it.

"How this all came to be, that's between you and me," he said. "Unless you've told someone…"

She shook her head, and he seemed a bit relieved. Not much, but some.

"So…you'll come stay with me?"

Everything inside her warned against even thinking about doing so.

"I can't afford not to do as you ask," she said softly, while her instincts continued to scream at her to find another way. She pushed through them. Forcing herself to focus on the facts, not feelings. Or imaginings. "I can't afford to hire protection. And I have to take extra precaution because of the baby…"

He took a step forward and she put up her hand. "I'm not happy about this. And the second they find whoever took a shot at me, I'm out of there," she said. "This isn't about us being together, in any way. It's nothing to do with us at all. Or to do with the fact that we're parents of the same child. I'm in danger. And you're trained to protect people. That's all it is."

She needed that firmly established. And though she hoped he never knew it, she was talking to herself as much as to him. The second he'd offered…she'd wanted to agree with his plan. Regardless of the fact he'd walked out on her, she still gravitated toward the man.

Whatever spell he'd cast the one night they'd been together had long-lasting effect. She took note. Promised herself she wouldn't forget for a second that the fantasy she'd built around them—around one true love—had come crashing painfully down.

"I'd stay here if it weren't for the baby," she added. And knew she was speaking the truth.

For all his earlier wordiness, Riley was suddenly quiet. Changing his mind?

She thought about herself actually in his home. She'd driven by it once, when she'd first begun to suspect she was pregnant. Had thought about telling him.

But she couldn't get over the way he'd callously walked out on her. After giving no indication, prior in the evening, that all he wanted was a one-night stand. To the contrary, when they'd talked about both liking jazz music, he'd said they'd have to take in a concert together sometime.

"What did your sisters say?" she asked, still leaning on the wall, though Aunt Blythe was going to be expecting her, with Blythe's packed bag, at Marge's house within the half hour. "About the baby?"

Riley shrugged. "I don't know."

"You don't know?" She stood up, faced him.

With a curious head tilt, almost like he was embarrassed, he said, "I walked out on them."

Oh.

So it wasn't just her.

He was that guy—the one who you couldn't count on to stick around. Period.

She gave him one last look, and then, without another word, went to pack the things her aunt had asked her to bring.

Chapter 10

Riley would have much preferred to take his SUV. Whoever was after Charlize likely knew what she drove, and wouldn't be as likely to recognize his vehicle. He posed the argument to Charlize as she returned with two suitcases in tow—one for her and one for her aunt, she'd said—and headed toward the back door where her car was parked in a detached garage.

He tried to take one of the bags for her. She shook her head, holding on to both handles, though she had to turn one back sideways to get them through the kitchen.

"I'll need my car where I'm staying," she'd said.

And out in the garage, when he suggested that he drive, as he had experience with defensive driving and fast speed chases, she declined once again.

"This way you can keep watch and be able to use

your gun," she'd replied, but he didn't think for a second she really expected that to happen.

She was letting him know that she was in control of her life, regardless of her need to stay with him. He got the message loud and clear. Respected her for it… and found it sexy.

So all the way to Lowell, he rode silently beside her, listening to her aunt chatter from the backseat, and keeping an eye out for any suspicious activity on the roads.

By the time they got to her aunt's house, he practically sprang from the vehicle. He did not make a good passenger. Never had. And opted to wait outside, pacing the sidewalk, while Charlize went inside with her family.

She'd said she was only coming to his place because of her need to protect the baby. Intimating that there was absolutely nothing between them. He wasn't so sure about that.

She was different. Not just as a person, but in his life. That one night…it had been like none other. More compelling, even, than those illicit nights with Marisol, his sometime partner at the FBI… He shoved those sensitive memories out of his mind.

And attraction aside, the baby Charlize was carrying, protecting, was his. That was a hell of a lot. No matter who raised the child.

Their families were forever, biologically, joined. And with his sisters, that meant they were joined emotionally, too. Any one of the Coltons would die for that child. Just as they'd die for each other.

Pulling out his phone he brought up his messaging

app, clicked on the group chat that included all five of his siblings and typed.

I apologize for my abrupt departure. At this time, I have no answers to your questions. Will provide them once I do. Someone has threatened Charlize's life. Shot at her this morning and missed. She will be staying at CI Headquarters until perp is caught. Don't make more of it than it is.

He didn't hit Send.

Didn't want them up in his space.

But they had to know. The woman would be staying at the headquarters of their family business.

Bailey and Ashanti. They'd have to know there'd be another person in the building.

Did they also have to know she was pregnant?

What if they heard her in the bathroom, being violently ill? He didn't want them calling 911 on her behalf.

The complications continued to pile up on him.

Charlize came out just as he was escalating to a whole new level of excess energy and he wasted no time getting back to the car, hitting Send on his text message before dropping his phone back in his pocket. "May I please drive?" he asked. It was her car. He couldn't demand.

He wouldn't beg.

"I have issues not driving when I'm in vehicles," he told her. She might as well know. "Never take cabs for that reason."

"What if you're traveling?"

"I rent cars."

She handed him the keys.

As tall as he was, he didn't have to adjust the seat much. One of the things he'd noticed during their night together. He and Charlize fit well.

"What about buses?" she asked as he turned onto the main road out of Lowell.

"I avoid them whenever possible."

Once they were on a country road, with long driveways up to homes that were mostly blocked from view by massive trees, Riley calmed down with every passing mile. And became aware of Charlize's silence, too. His brain back in full gear, focused on the task at hand, a list took place in his mind's eye. Immediate considerations.

They were going home together, to his place. Where they'd be living together, at least for a day or two.

The idea of sharing space with her didn't fragment his control again. Didn't even send up negative vibes.

Interesting.

But then, he knew it wasn't forever. Or even for very long.

"I cook on Sundays." He offered pertinent information. "Various meals. They're marked and dated and in individual vacuum-sealed bags in the freezer. You're welcome to any of them, and anything else in the house you might need or want," he said. "And don't worry, you're not infringing or putting me out. My siblings have no qualms about helping themselves so I've learned just to keep things stocked. Half the stuff, I don't even like."

That might be a bit of an exaggeration, but not by much. Some weeks he'd be fine with peanut butter, a loaf of bread and beer.

"Thank you."

"It's after five and I'm sure you need to eat," he continued, traveling a conversational path that didn't seem to bring any qualms from within. "I've got lasagna, vegetable soup, bourbon pork and chicken marsala, for sure." He pictured the interior of his freezer. "And there are meatballs and several things of spaghetti sauce. The spaghetti's in the cupboard. I have a microwave container that cooks it up quickly..." Being a good host was something he'd learned young. It wasn't something you forgot, even if you preferred not to exercise the talent.

"The veggies are all done separately," he continued. "In their own bags, and marked. You can choose what you want to go with whatever main dish." The girls each had their own preferences and dislikes. And it was just easiest to feed them what they liked.

"And the veggie bin in the refrigerator is always filled with fresh produce."

She was staring at him.

"What?" he asked.

"I'm trying to picture you pushing around a full cart in the grocery store..."

He wondered if she liked the image. And immediately disavowed it. "I don't," he quickly assured her, lest she build him into some kind of family man he was not.

"JJ, my housekeeper, does it. Twice a week. I'm a run in and run out kind of guy, if it's a last minute thing, and I have no other option. She cleans, too. On Fridays." Which was coming up.

He'd need to let JJ know he had a houseguest...

"There are three bedrooms upstairs," he said. "All large enough to be a small apartment. I'm in the master at the end of the hall. You can have your pick of either of the other two. The downstairs bedroom has been converted to a filing and storage room for the business. You'll have your own bathroom."

Lest she think there would be forced intimacies in their near future. Or feared that he'd be planning on them.

He was ten minutes from home. Just one more thing to cover.

"As the father of the child you're carrying, I'm hiring myself as your private bodyguard until this is over," he said, choosing his words carefully. He wasn't up for being flexible on this one. "Inside, you're on your own, but when you need to leave, go to work, whatever, that baby has my protection. As a hired professional, I'll make myself available to you as needed, on your schedule." His laptop was state-of-the-art, his Wi-Fi excellent and he had the best unlimited data plan and phone hotspot on the market. He could do his research from anywhere.

He could see her looking at him. Peripheral vision didn't provide much opportunity for accurate expression reading. So he prepared for whatever argument she might bring.

He was right on this one. And...

"You could have just offered," she said after a long minute had passed. "I'd much rather have a gun beside me, than not, at the moment."

Well, then. There you go.

Maybe life didn't have to be so complicated, after all.

She didn't feel safe out and about alone.

She hated being afraid. Hated letting fear win in any

capacity. But she'd nearly been run over by a truck. She'd been shot at.

Only a fool ignored the warnings.

Giving in to them, quitting her job since they didn't know which case was posing the threat, was not an option. Evil didn't get to win.

But she had to take care. And didn't have money to hire her own bodyguard. Most particularly not with a baby on the way.

Riley's solution eased some of the tension that had been building within her.

And, as she took out her phone to avoid any further conversation between them in the car, checked her email, and saw that she'd had a response from her doctor's office regarding an appointment, his solution brought a whole new realm of agitation.

Not anything she was going to tend to trapped in the confines of a moving vehicle.

Later, though, after she'd carried her own suitcase upstairs, having taken it from him as he'd lifted it out of the car, spent as much time as she reasonably could getting settled into the huge room farthest from his upstairs, she had to go back downstairs.

Deal with Riley.

And the situation they'd unknowingly created.

He wasn't in the main office as she came down the stairs. Nor was he in the dining room as she passed through on her way to the kitchen. If she wasn't in danger, she'd head out to get something to eat. But if she wasn't in danger, she wouldn't be there at all.

She pulled open the freezer. Tried to pretend to herself that she wasn't curious to try Riley's cooking, but the truth was, she wanted to try it all. Loved the idea of him keeping homemade meals stocked in the freezer for his grown siblings.

For a guy who'd sworn off marriage and family, he sure didn't act the part. He hadn't been kidding; the freezer was filled to the hilt, all with vacuum bags shelved by type, and clearly labeled. As she read, the choice got harder to make. So much of it sounded good.

Had he eaten? Should she make something for him, too? It would be rude not to do so. And yet, would it be too much like they were living together, rather than just staying in the same place, if they sat down to dinner together?

Where was he? Maybe there was a family room somewhere. Or a finished basement...

"The bourbon pork is the girls' favorite." She'd barely registered footsteps when he spoke.

"They're hardly girls, Riley," she said, to cover her abrupt switch from her appreciation of his caring nature back to the reality of standing in a virtual stranger's kitchen perusing his freezer contents.

Try as she might, though, she couldn't make Riley feel like someone she hardly knew. Instead, she continued to have the sense that she'd known of him forever.

"They're all professionals with careers. Grown women."

"I diapered all four of them. They'll always be girls to me."

With a sudden bout of deflation sliding over her, she pulled out a bag of pork. "Do you want one?" she asked.

"Yeah. And some of that broccoli and a baked potato, too. The potato is great with the bourbon juices.

All the alcohol's been cooked out of the sauce, just in case you were wondering."

Looking for a baked potato, she stood there, until Riley reached around her, pulling out two bags of cut up white cubes.

She'd been about to fix dinner, and ended up collecting plates and silverware as Riley just set about doing what needed to be done to get their food on the table. He knew the microwave settings. Exactly how long everything took to reheat without overheating. The potatoes went in foil in a toaster oven set to broil.

"I eat in here," he said as she headed toward the dining room table through the kitchen archway. The alcove he pointed to on the far end of the kitchen held an old Formica-topped table, square, with four padded chairs.

The man definitely had his ways. "Any particular chair?"

He pointed to a chair that backed to the wall with one hand as he pulled the potatoes out of the toaster oven with a mitt on the other, and she found herself imagining a much younger Riley at that table. In that kitchen. And saw a sudden vision of her own child there. With him. And not her.

Debating about whether or not she should sit with him, or take her food up to her room with her, Charlize knew she really had little choice.

They had a matter to discuss, whether he was going to like it or not.

She decided to wait until they were almost done eating—which they were doing in complete silence. No point in ruining a perfectly fine appetite with such incredibly good food on the table.

"I'm too old to be a father." He'd taken a sip of the

beer he'd pulled from the refrigerator. She'd opted for a bottle of spring water. Almost choked on the swallow she tried to take after he'd spoken.

"I don't know what to say to that," she told him when her throat was clear enough to speak. "Of course, you aren't, but I'm guessing you aren't really talking about years.

"In my experience, and I've got a lot of it, the healthy state of a family isn't based on the parents' ages—at least, not entirely. Obviously, some younger parents maybe wouldn't have the struggles they do if they were a bit more mature, or wouldn't have them to the same extent. But a person's ability to love, to guide, to set and maintain boundaries, to discipline, to teach, and, to *love*, isn't bound by age." She put extra emphasis as she repeated the most important quality to happy family life—love.

"I've had a lot of years to develop my particular habits. I'm set in my ways. And I'm grouchy when I have to be flexible."

Like avoiding the passenger side of any vehicle. He'd handled the situation just fine. So he wasn't telling her the real problem. He wasn't talking to one of his sisters, or a client or law-enforcement peer. He had a counselor at the table. One who was pretty adept at knowing when to hold her tongue.

Dinner was almost done. She still had that matter to discuss. Didn't want to think about it. The discussion, or the actual event.

"If we were to ever go out with the kid together, you know to a teacher conference or sporting event, people would think I'm the grandfather."

"You're only thirteen years older than I am, Riley,

not thirty. And you're in better shape at forty-three than a lot of the fathers I visit who are my age. You've got an added maturity and wisdom that any child would be lucky to benefit from…" Because they were talking about him being a father, not them being a couple.

The former was happening. The latter was very firmly not. No matter how succinctly her subconscious kept remembering his lovemaking.

"Say we have a boy," she started, and noticed him flinch at the word *we*. Almost let her thought trail away unspoken, and then chose not to do so. "Say he plays football. You'd be fifty-eight or so if he makes varsity. I'd be willing to bet my life's savings that you'd still be able to outthrow him, and catch him on the field, too. Assuming disaster hasn't struck before then."

He glanced up at that, frowning. "What? Disaster? Who goes around making room for disaster?"

Smiling, she nodded. "Exactly," she said. "Anything can happen to anyone at any age, in terms of physical disabilities or death. We don't live our lives looking for either. Most of us live our lives hoping that they'll be long and fruitful. And it happens more times than not. A good majority of us live to old age. So with that in mind, and with today's longer life spans, this child will have gray hair by the time you're heading out."

Putting his fork and knife in the middle of his empty plate, Riley didn't respond verbally or in his expression.

He stood, reached for her empty plate, carried them both to the sink. And when he came back for her silverware, said, "I'm closing in on half a century of living. I'm set in my ways."

Leaving her to decipher the message she was supposed to take from that. Was he telling her he wasn't going to be a father to the child they'd created?

Or just stating a fact she was going to have to learn to live with?

Maybe he was just reiterating that there was no hope for the two of them as a real family.

He needn't have worried on that count.

Riley figured his handling of the dishes, combined with his surly mood, would be cue enough for Charlize to clear out of the kitchen. She continued to haunt him with the scent of her shampoo. And the beating of her heart in his personal space.

He could almost feel the palpitation. And the air she breathed in and out of that gorgeous body of hers. He'd been adamant about his right to protect his child. Pretty much left her no choice but to move in with him. Had been completely certain he was absolutely right in his insistence.

And he'd been wrong.

Having Charlize Kent in his personal space had not been a good choice. Having any woman there would have been an oddity. He'd never, ever brought a girlfriend or fling home to CI headquarters. Or the family home when it had been that.

Not ever.

Charlize's presence in the space made things complicated again. *Too* complicated.

He wanted her; the chemistry between them as explosive as a match to gasoline. Had to stand at the sink after the dishes were in the dishwasher to keep his hard-on from becoming another unspoken conversation between them.

"I have a doctor's appointment in the morning."

Or…an announcement from her could shrink his penis right up.

Of course she'd have called her doctor. She was three months pregnant. And he, in all his smartness, had insisted on accompanying her every single place she went.

"They're going to be doing an ultrasound, since I'm already starting my fourth month. The appointment will last about an hour. You can wait, or you can drop me off and pick me up afterward."

Her dismissal of him, speaking of his presence there like it was no more than taking care of her, acting like the whole thing was no big deal…kind of pissed him off.

Whether it made logical sense or not, he didn't like feeling dismissed. His phone vibrated in his pocket. Again. The fifth time since he'd texted his siblings. As he'd done with all the rest, he ignored it.

"As the father of the child, I'd like to hear what the doctor has to say," he blurted, as much out of perverseness than anything else, he supposed. "And… I'd like to be present for the ultrasound." Marisol had talked about her husband having been in the room when they'd found out they were having a girl…the conversation had been pertinent because she'd been missing her son so acutely one night…

He turned from the sink at Charlize's silence. In the middle of the kitchen, halfway between the refrigerator and him, she stood, mouth open.

His bad mood dissipated way too quickly at the sight of that mouth. Yeah, because it looked so tempting and kissable, but more because he'd managed to make her speechless.

She wasn't as unaffected by him as she pretended.

It was almost enough to make him take back his ultrasound statement. Yet, he didn't. He'd never been to an ultrasound before. Was a bit curious.

And as Charlize continued to stand there as though she'd just heard the worst news of her life, he softened, no fractiousness left at all. "I'm not trying to make more between us than what's there, or insinuate myself into your life. I'm not even sure I'm insinuating myself into the child's life. I'd just like to be there for the ultrasound." But it wasn't nonnegotiable. "If that's okay with you," he added, to make that clear.

She closed her mouth. Studied him for a moment, and then nodded. "Yes, of course that's okay," she said. "As you say, the baby is your child, too."

With that, she passed by him, left the kitchen and a few seconds later he heard her feet climbing the stairs. She'd gone without leaving the kiss on his lips he so desperately wanted.

Whether she'd be back down, or had locked herself in her room and would remain quiet enough that he shouldn't know she was there, didn't matter. She could be invisible and completely silent and he'd still feel her. Still want her.

And still not want a marriage and family of his own.

Heading into his office, Riley hoped to God he could lose himself in work. He hoped for a lot of things.

While the only thing he knew for certain, was that it was going to be one hell of a long night.

Chapter 11

Charlize slept all night. She didn't toss and turn. Didn't have any dreams that she remembered. Didn't even wake up once before dawn. She'd expected to lie awake, at least until she heard Riley Colton come upstairs, and then to fight memories of the night they'd spent several hours in bed together. Expected to have to fight off her mind's attempts to re-create the fantasy world she'd grown up in and had thought he'd completed.

Instead, she'd lain down just before nine, with her plugged-in phone in hand and a puzzle game pulled up, and had woken ten hours later with her phone on the mattress beside her.

She'd never heard Riley come upstairs. Didn't know if he was up yet.

And didn't want to run into him in the hall on her

way to the shower. But she had to pee. Grabbing a couple of the saltine crackers she'd brought from home and laid on the nightstand beside her before crawling into bed, she munched as she slipped out of her nightie and back into the light blue pants and white shirt she'd had on the day before, grabbed her toiletry bag and a pair of light blue skinny jeans and another short-sleeved, tailored white top, along with undies and, arms full, peeked her head out the door.

Silence met her. Hoping Riley was already downstairs, and not lying naked in all his sexy gloriousness in bed just a few doors away, she slipped quietly across the hall, into the bathroom, and locked the door behind her.

As it turned out, she didn't see Riley until five minutes before they had to leave for the doctor's appointment. She'd heard his voice coming from a room just off the huge main office area as she'd made herself some toast and poured a glass of juice for breakfast. And she'd smiled at Ashanti, who was sitting at a huge L-shaped desk with multiple computer screens, her long braids hanging over the shoulders of her pantsuit.

The CI tech expert hadn't seemed surprised to see her. Which likely meant that Riley had filled in his colleagues and siblings on her temporary presence in their abode. Had he told his employees about the baby, too?

Or the woman's smile could have meant that she was used to seeing female strangers coming downstairs in the morning…

Already dismissing the thought, she was distracted from it as Riley came out of the room off the main office.

"You ready to go?" he asked. His beard was looking a little tamer than usual—maybe because he'd recently come from the shower?

The thought brought images of his naked body that she most definitely couldn't ponder over, and instead, her gaze was caught by the vivid intensity in his bright blue eyes. The man lit her up. Whether he was naked, or fully clothed and heading out the door.

Not a comforting realization.

One more thing to deal with.

She glanced behind him. "What's in there?" She hadn't even walked into the office portion of the house. Just passed it.

"My office. It used to be my father's study," he said as he led them through the kitchen and out to his SUV.

The comment brought her up short again. For as much as Riley Colton didn't see himself as a family man, he seemed to have planted himself right in the very core of all the family he'd ever known.

How did you hate a guy like that?

Or even continue to resent him?

The couple-mile ride to her clinic was quick—and passed uncomfortably as she kept a close eye out for any activity that looked at all suspicious. A person sitting in a parked car. Or someone scary-looking walking on the sidewalk.

For any black trucks at all. New. Old. Big. Small.

Riley asked her to stay seated as he parked next to the building, and then came around to stand guard at the door as she got out of his SUV. He kept himself at her back, with only the building in front of them until they were inside, and then still stood behind her at the desk, listening as she gave her name, watching as she signed in.

And when they were asked to take seats, he chose ones in the corner, with the backs to the wall, away from the one set of windows farther down the room. He seemed at ease. Nonthreatening. Had even untucked his polo shirt, leaving it loose to cover the gun he wore.

"How'd you sleep?" He asked the first personal question of the day.

"Great," she told him, still marveling at how she'd just dropped right off and slept all night. The bed was comfortable, but it had been more than that. It was like all of her worries and responsibilities had just slipped away for those hours.

Because Riley was there to watch over them? And her?

He seemed restless once they sat down. Lifting his ankle across his knee. Then dropping it. Smoothing his hand down one thigh. Then the other. Leaning on one side of the chair with his elbow, then the other. He didn't pull out a phone. Didn't occupy himself as the two women in the room, farther down and out of earshot, were doing.

He was making her nervous. The exam itself wouldn't be comfortable, and she'd probably need a prenatal vitamin prescription, too. And the ultrasound…her entire body buzzed with nervous energy every time she thought about it. Her stomach started to churn and she wasn't sure how much longer she could just sit there.

Was she having twins? They ran in Riley's family.

"I've always wanted kids," she finally said, needing to feel relevant, like the moment wasn't time out of time, but her new reality. Like she belonged in that room with two other pregnant women.

"Kids?" he asked. "As in plural?"

She nodded, knowing he wouldn't get it, wouldn't agree. But not at all apologetic for how she felt. With all that she was going through, that they were facing, so much of it out of her control, speaking her own truth, being completely honest, was paramount.

"I was an only child," she told him. "And while I was greatly loved, and always felt safe and special, I was also lonely a lot, too."

Twins would take care of that.

And be double the work for a working single mother. Still...

"Because your mother wasn't around," Riley inserted, more statement than question.

"And because I never knew my father," she pointed out. "But I had my grandparents to fill those holes, at least in large part. And my aunts, too. But there was never anyone like me at home, you know? No one to play with, tell secrets to, or get in trouble with. Christmas morning I was the only kid, the only one antsy with excitement..."

He groaned. "I was, too, for a long time."

She looked over at him. Wondered what he was thinking. And really thought about how his life had changed so drastically when he was more than halfway grown up. Tried to remember herself as a teen. Would she have welcomed a baby then?

She was pretty sure she'd have been overjoyed...

He hadn't said anything more. And she wasn't okay with the silence.

"Didn't you ever get lonely?" she asked him. "Those first thirteen years?"

He shook his head. "With my dad's career, and

politics…my folks were always so busy. Back then I got to go with them a lot of the time…"

"A kid living in an adult world." Sounded lonely to her. "What about at home?"

A shrug was his only answer.

"I don't want my child to grow up lonely." It mattered that he know that. At first, she didn't get why, but when she sat there, nervous and being oddly calmed by his warmth next to her, too, she figured it out.

No matter what happened between her and Riley, even if they were able to co-parent their child somehow, no matter how much they might be attracted to each other, there was no future for them. He wasn't a man who'd want more kids in the future.

Of course, he might not be attracted to her at all anymore. He hadn't given her any real indication that he was.

But something told her that he wanted her. A vibe. A sense. Something.

Self-preservation, most likely. The knowledge was there to warn her of the danger.

If she didn't want her heart stomped on a second time, she had to stay away from him.

Riley waited while Charlize went back for a physical with her doctor. He kept a trained eye on the room. On what he could see of the parking lot outside. But didn't figure any of Charlize's clients would figure her for an OB/GYN appointment.

He was confident they hadn't been followed to the clinic.

But he wasn't going to get complacent. Not for a second.

He'd lost a loved one once to the evil in society. He wasn't about to lose his child, or its mother, to them. Marisol had lost a lot, too, before she'd been killed.

He'd spoken with Iglesias that morning. There was nothing new to report on Charlize's case. The bullet they'd pulled from her town house was too common to trace, from a make of gun that was sold commonly all over the state. Michigan was a hunting state. Guns were as prevalent as ice cream. Iglesias had expressed again his relief that Riley had Charlize at his place, and told him to watch his back.

"We're dealing with a firecracker," Iglesias had said. "Someone with anger issues acting on a surplus of emotion. Someone who's not too smart, who won't probably weigh the consequences of a stupid action."

Riley knew the type.

In terms of Wes Matthews and Capital X, the detective had spoken with Police Chief Andrew Fox, and everyone was frustrated with how little there was to go on. All the investors who'd already reported to the police had provided cash transfers that couldn't be traced. Riley had Ashanti trying, anyway.

And Brody... Riley pulled out his phone. Checked both email and text. Nothing from Brody. But there were a couple of pertinent pieces of information from Ashanti and Bailey regarding the cold case.

He'd avoided the group chat with siblings. Hadn't opened it to read any of the seven responses he'd received. He'd said he'd get to them when he had answers and he would.

But it was a new day. And they used that same thread sometimes to check in with any updates on current CI cases. Most particularly if they were engaged in day job activities and couldn't make phone calls to everyone.

He pushed to open the thread.

The first four replies were emojis only. A thumbs-up. Two that had hearts. And one with a worried-looking face. Or maybe it was consternation. Frustration. Who could tell with those damned things?

The fifth was a message from Griffin.

We've got you.

That was unexpected.

Pushing back against a surge of emotion he didn't know how to handle, and most particularly not in a semi-public place, he scrolled down to the most recent two messages, coming in back to back that morning.

Sadie hadn't found anything on the scientist yet.

And Griffin was going to be in court all morning, so out of pocket.

While he'd been debating whether to respond to any of the texts, or continue to hold his silence until he had something pertinent to say, the door had opened and his name had been called.

He had no reason to be uptight walking down that hall. The medical procedure was information gathering only. They knew there was a baby. He assumed it was healthy. And yet, he was sweating as he walked into the dimly lit exam room, and took his place up by Charlize's left shoulder as instructed.

If nothing else, she was safe there. The thought calmed him.

And then he glanced toward her exposed, still flat, stomach. Remembering…way, way too much. The scent of that skin. The taste of it. How it had cradled his penis as he'd slid down her…and again, later, as she'd slid up him…

"This is going to be cold," the technician, a middle-aged woman, said.

And Riley finally looked at Charlize's face, saw her looking, not at the tech, or the blank gray screen off to their left, but at him.

Their gazes locked. With a peculiar recognition he couldn't explain or deny, he suddenly realized he knew her. *Really* knew her. And accepted that she knew him.

Not just physically, though there was definitely that, too. Intimately. Emotionally…

And then, the technician directed their attention to the screen.

"Twins run in his family," Charlize blurted, her voice filled with emotion he couldn't decipher. The words brought a fresh wave of cold sweats and he stared at the moving gray shadows on that screen, trying to pick out anything that looked human among them.

"There's the head." With one hand controlling the camera she'd been gliding along Charlize's bared midsection, the technician touched the screen with the other.

He saw it. A head. Heart pounding, he stared. Clearly saw the head. And from there he could make out the neck. And legs and…

"How big is it?" he asked, completely stupefied at the moment. If his mother had ever had ultrasounds, he didn't remember hearing about it. Or seeing the film.

The tech had been zeroing in on different things.

Seeming to take separate images. "Three and a half inches," she said.

How could a human possibly measure less than four inches?

"Your doctor will give you the full report as soon as we're done here and she's had a chance to look at the imaging," the technician continued. "And I'm making copies for both of you to take, as well."

He opened his mouth to say that he wouldn't need any. But didn't get the words out. His sisters might want to see them.

Or…he didn't know. Just kept staring. Watching the movement. Trying to figure out how that tiny little being *could* move. Wondering who would protect it if it got picked on when it started school…

An inane thought…

"There's definitely only one," Charlize said. She sounded disappointed. And he remembered her conversation from earlier. Wanting more than one baby.

"Yep," the technician said.

He wanted to tell her she had a lot of time to have her other children. Didn't like how that felt when he thought about it. Looked at the screen again.

Just…wow. He couldn't get over how small that being was, and imagined how much work it had ahead of it in the coming months.

"Can you tell if it's a boy or a girl?" he asked. Not his gig, really. He was only a bystander at the moment. With some sort of commitment. And sisters and a brother who…

What?

How could they all be a family? He and Charlize weren't even a couple…

"Your doctor will discuss all that with you," the woman said. "But just from personal experience, I don't see anything that tells either way. It's usually eighteen to twenty-two weeks before an ultrasound will show. You're at what? Thirteen weeks?"

Riley drew his eyes from the screen for a quick glance to see Charlize nod. And then resumed his suddenly panic-filled viewing.

He didn't want to take on fatherhood. Not now. Not with...

"Okay, let's get the heartbeat up here..."

Before he'd had time to compute, to follow along, the room filled with sound. Rapid tattoos. Kind of a heartbeat rhythm, but much more rapid than he'd expected.

A whole new panic suffused him, making him almost nauseated. The baby's heart wasn't right. Oh, God, no. That tiny little thing...

Why wasn't the technician running for help? Sounding alarm bells. Poised to leave the room himself, to yell for someone to come running, he heard Charlize's voice as though through a muffle. Or far away.

"It's so fast..."

"Yeah, that's normal," the technician said and Riley felt so weak he could hardly keep himself upright.

He did. Riley Colton didn't give in to weakness. Of any kind.

But he had to stand still for a second or two. Breathe. And let the relief wash over him.

Chapter 12

Charlize needed to go home. She had some things to pick up, her blow-dryer for one. And some different clothes. She'd packed in such a hurry the day before she'd just grabbed and thrown in.

Those things were the excuse she gave Riley for needing to stop by her house after they left the clinic. But the deeper truth was that she needed to breathe in her own space for a few minutes. To look at the room upstairs that was going to become a nursery. To walk where she was going to be living, as the realization of what was happening to her sank in.

She was going to be a mother.

Already was a mother.

That picture on the screen, the sound of the heartbeat filling the room, had solidified in her mind what her body had already known.

She had become a different person, forever. Fantasy-land as she'd always lived it, believed in it, waited for it, was gone forever. She wasn't married to the love of her life, having their child.

She was a single mother, having her own child.

And she wanted it more than she'd ever imagined. She needed a few minutes in her own space to absorb it all. The feelings. The changes.

To accept them. Take them on. To begin the new journey.

She let Riley practically wrap himself around her as he walked her to the car, with not only his back half covering hers, a leg insinuated between hers, as though they were dancing, her back to his front. He had an arm around her shoulder, too, as though ready to push away anyone who might could come at her that way.

"Duck your head into me," he said, his voice not quite urgent, but deadly serious, and she did as he'd instructed, heart pounding. She was not going to lose her new life just as it was beginning.

She was not.

When she was safely in the vehicle, and saw him come around and get in, rather than go chasing after someone, she asked, "Did you see something?"

"No," he said. "But I didn't see a shooter yesterday morning, either."

Of course he hadn't. He'd been in the house, behind her.

And…crazy hard to believe that the shooting had just been the day before. She'd moved out of her house. Slept in a new bed. Seen her entire life change before her eyes that morning. The shooting…seemed part of a distant past.

Funny, though, that her night in the hotel room with Riley didn't seem that way. If anything, it seemed more recent than all the weeks it had been.

He didn't drive straight to her house, saying he wanted to check out the neighborhoods first. And make certain they weren't being followed.

She wanted to know what he thought about the morning. They'd just witnessed the miracle of life. A life they'd created together. And he hadn't said a word.

"I can't believe how formed the baby was," she said when she couldn't sit silently with their miracle unspoken between them. "I was expecting to see something more like a peanut, not be able to make out an actual facial structure, and torso and legs..."

"I feel that I should warn you," Riley started, and she almost told him just to stop. Wanted to put her hands over her ears. He had to do what he had to. Reject his part in it if he must, but she didn't want to hear it right then. Not yet...

"In light of what's going on, the danger you're in, that after what I saw this morning, I'm going to be hovering close until we find who's out to get you, and I know the guy's safely behind bars."

Oh.

"I'm not going to be able to step back, to give you space. You have a right to it, I understand that. But..." He shook his head. "I just don't see it happening."

She smiled. She just couldn't help it, even while she warned herself not to make too much of the ownership he was showing over their child. He'd never denied responsibility. Or a willingness to provide for the child. "We both want the same thing, Riley," she told him quietly as she sobered. "To keep this baby safe. I'm grateful for your protection."

He glanced her way, but only briefly. She got a glimpse of those striking blue eyes, just not enough of one to read anything in them. When he turned in a direction opposite of her house—and CI headquarters, too—she immediately tensed and asked, "Is someone following us?"

"No. I'm just being diligent." He told her he'd spoken with Iglesias that morning, repeated what the detective had told him about her shooter being unpredictable. One who might act stupidly. Which made him that much harder to protect against. The guy could try anything, out in plain sight.

"Chances are, he doesn't know my vehicle," he said then. "It's lucky that both times I was at your place, I walked there. I'm planning to park on the street behind your town house and cut through the backyard. But we'll drive the street a time or two first, to make certain there's no one lurking there."

He glanced her way again. Circling through neighborhoods slowly, mostly keeping an eye on the road and their surroundings.

She appreciated his keeping her apprised. But when it came to keeping them safe, she trusted him to know his stuff.

He got them inside the town house, through the back door safely. Easily. So much so that she began to hope that maybe all the precaution was overkill. And yet, she was still grateful for it. If ever there was a time designed to fit "better safe than sorry" that was it.

She was upstairs, a second suitcase open, more carefully selecting what she might need over the next few days, adding some shadows and eyeliner and some earrings to her growing stack, when she heard the front door open. Moving to the wall, she waited, inched her way until she could at least partially see out the window. Her heart pounded and she told herself she had to get the fear in check.

She wanted to call out to Riley but didn't want to give away her location, or even the knowledge that she was in the house, if someone besides him was inside.

Where was he? Outside? Had he seen something? Heard something?

How did people live with their lives in constant danger?

Riley had talked about his life with the FBI the night of the fundraiser. About how it felt to make a difference to the world of crime threatening the nation. He'd made mention of having made enemies. He'd been talking about how rusty he was at attending formal, "feel-good" functions, having traded the social culture of his youth for the darkest opposite—chasing down the drug lords and cartel members that were a continued threat.

The front door closed.

Afraid to move away from the wall in her own house, Charlize couldn't really even imagine how he'd lived for more than twenty years with the knowledge that at any time someone he was closing in on could get him first. Or someone he'd put away could get out and come find him.

"I'm coming up." Riley's voice.

"Okay," she called back. And moved away from the wall. Feeling foolish. As she heard his footsteps getting closer, she closed the lid of her rolling bag. No point in having intimates right there for them both to stare at.

If she'd thought about it, or been in her right mind, she'd have wondered why he'd felt a need to visit her in her bedroom. As it was, the first warning she had was the look on his face.

It was grim. The corners of his mouth tight inside his beard.

In his hand he held a box, a small brown package. "This was on the side of the front porch."

"What is that?" she asked, looking inside. And then up at him. "Is that one of those toy confetti poppers?"

He nodded. And turned the box so she could read what had been crudely written on the left inner side. *I told you to call them off Next time this explosion won't be fake.*

The letters were black. Bold. There was no punctuation.

"Do you think they'll be able to ID him off it?" she asked, too horrified to let herself fully comprehend that someone who wanted her dead had been at her home since she'd left the evening before.

There and wanting her dead.

"I doubt it," Riley said. "He's dumb, but he probably wore gloves. The good news, if you can call it that, is that this tells us that the perp is likely one of the guys Iglesias visited yesterday. He didn't tell you to stay away this time. He said call 'them' off. Iglesias's visit pissed him off."

She nodded. Not liking what she was about to say, but knowing it was right. "So we keep after them, force their hand," she said.

"Iglesias and his guys keep after them," he told her.

"I'm not going to desert my clients," she told Riley. "I'll stay away physically, because of the baby, but

I've built rapport with those families. I could be their only hope…"

All of her visits weren't in-home. She had phone calls. Video calls. "I've canceled my physical appointments for the rest of the week. I did that yesterday afternoon. Rescheduled them for next week. But I can compel my clients to put me on video call and show me around the house, just like I could check out the house on a personal visit. It's not ideal. Not as good as being there, but for a few days it can work."

He nodded. Didn't argue. Wasn't trying to talk her out of doing what she needed to do.

And she needed him to know, "I really want this baby." The words, when she heard them aloud, didn't sound like enough. Didn't in any way communicate the new dimension that had just entered her heart. Showing her a wealth of love she hadn't known existed. "I'm happy about it. Excited. And scared to death that something could happen to it," she told him. "Whatever it takes to keep the baby safe… I'm on board with it."

"Iglesias is sending someone over to pick up the box," he said, standing in her bedroom as though he'd been there many times.

Belonged there.

"It might be a bit."

She nodded. Wanted him to come in. And to go. The battle raged inside her and there was no clear winner. With his free hand he reached out to her face, cupped it, caressed her jawbone—and she wasn't going to tell him no.

Right or wrong.

His hand dropped to his side and she was bereft.

And relieved, too. As much as her body craved

more satisfaction from his, the hurt from the way he'd walked out on her still stung.

And with a baby coming, she couldn't just think about herself. About what she wanted in the moment.

"I loved a woman once."

She froze, her hand on the top of the closed suitcase. If she moved, would he go? If she didn't, would he tell her more?

She looked up at him. Met his gaze. Held on for as long as he'd let her.

"She was a fellow agent, a member of my team," he said. "We were partnered more often than not. It worked because we were both married to the job. Spouses and family weren't an issue."

Was. At the moment, that word was louder in her mind than any other. Was this relationship permanently in the past, like the word he used indicated?

The way he held himself, not quite defensively, but almost as though he was daring anyone to pass any judgment on what he had to say, told Charlize a lot. She was trained to catch behavioral nuances, to know as much from what she observed as she did from what she heard.

Riley Colton might look casual standing in that doorway, but there was nothing casual about what he was telling her.

What he was telling her was significant.

What it meant, she had yet to know.

"Her name was Marisol."

There was that word—*was*—again.

She continued to look him in the eye, but otherwise, didn't move. He had her full focus. It seemed important that he know that.

"She'd been married, but her dedication to the job had ultimately broken up her marriage. She couldn't leave the job. Not so much the FBI. She could have left the bureau, maybe. But fighting injustice against others, facing the bad guys and taking them down…" He shook his head. "She couldn't leave that."

Just as he couldn't. She was getting his message but her heart had to know.

"She could only handle the fear of living in a world of criminals if she was actively out there fighting them."

She nodded. Sensed there was more. Waited.

If she had to hear it, she wanted it over with. Quickly.

"She had a son…"

Oh, God. No. She had to consciously stop the shake of her head that was her natural reaction. The muscles in her neck tight, she forced herself to remain still.

"After the divorce, her husband had full custody and it ate at her every day to know that their child was better off with him than with her. Ate at her that she wasn't the mother he needed. She missed him like crazy…"

The road she'd thought they were on had just taken a turn. Were they talking about why he wouldn't get married?

Or was this about their baby and his not knowing how to be a father or doubting the kind of father he could be?

Nuances. She had to read between the lines.

"She had him on her days off. The arrangement was amicable, but it was anguish for her, too," Riley continued, still standing in the middle of the doorway. Still holding the box.

"We caught this case…it ended up bigger than we'd

imagined…instead of a local drug bust, we ended up part of an international investigation, taking down an organization that ran more drugs and guns than either of us had ever seen. It had major holdings in Michigan. And there was a kingpin here, too. The guy found out about her ex-husband and son. Threatened them. If she didn't lose some key evidence, they were going to kill her family…"

The *was* screamed loudly now. She braced herself.

"She screwed up. To save her family, she screwed up. And got herself killed."

Charlize had known no happy ending was coming. Tried to swallow, but her throat was too dry. Ironically, there was enough moisture for tears to spring to her eyes.

"I'm so sorry," she said, mostly in a whisper.

Chin jutting, he nodded. Took a step back.

"I can't risk having a family," he said.

Actually, he was already doing it. Any one of his siblings could be in danger. But one thing she knew—and knew loud and clear. It wasn't healthy for someone to settle for something they knew wasn't right for them, to talk themselves into a relationship when they really didn't want one. Whether Riley's feelings were based on reality or just his perceived reality really didn't matter. What mattered was that he didn't want a relationship.

And now she knew why.

"Your job…this danger you're in…it's an anomaly," he said, still looking straight at her. She frowned, not sure where he was going with what he was saying.

"Mostly you're helping people find a way to have the healthy lives they want. And when you're not, when you're trying to get a woman out of a dangerous situation, or taking children from a home, you don't actually do the taking. The police and the courts do that. And the perpetrators are generally regular guys, albeit with anger or drug issues, not hardened criminals. What's happening here—" he held up the box "—isn't an everyday thing in the life of a social worker. This is a guy who's off his rocker. And who doesn't even have the wherewithal to back off when he knows the police are involved. It makes him more dangerous until we get him, but it doesn't make your job more dangerous in the long haul."

What he said made sense. And made her feel a little better, too. Even knowing the danger wasn't gone yet. He'd put an end date on him acting as her protector, while, without even realizing it, she'd begun to feel permanently threatened.

"Your job won't put that baby at risk on a daily basis. My past will."

And his present could, too. She understood.

Could have argued, at least could have given him another side to think about. The chances of them getting in a car accident were greater than someone coming after Riley's family, now that he was no longer with the FBI. But she didn't.

Nodding, Charlize turned away, grabbed a sweater out of the closet to offset the air-conditioned chill in Riley's house.

When she turned back, he was gone.

Chapter 13

As soon as Charlize headed upstairs at his place, Riley called Bailey, who had the goal of becoming an FBI agent, and asked him to head back and work from CI headquarters because he needed to go out for a bit. In the meantime, he had to help his houseguest set up to work.

She was in her room, door closed, and he knocked. Entered only when he was told he could do so. And found her with her laptop case on the bed, a plug-in charger beside it.

He looked at the case. Not the bed. And knew he had to get out of there.

To focus on the outside dangers threatening her. And Brody.

Not on the intimate ones trying to take place right there in that room. Not even his siblings knew the details about Marisol. He'd poured his heart out and couldn't get it back in the container he held so carefully around it. And had no plan to go forward with it out there.

How did he proceed without a plan?

Way more important, how did he be a father and keep his child safe?

"The fact that they left the warning on your porch is good news in one sense," he told Charlize, a bit awkwardly, out of nowhere, as he cleared off the small desk in the room she'd chosen and gave her the Wi-Fi information. His thoughts had to remain on keeping her safe. And finding Wes Matthews and Capital X so that he could get Brody home. He did not need to be aware of her sweet scent in a bedroom in his home.

"How so?" she asked, setting her laptop on the cleared desk and opening it up. Paper files came out of the laptop case next, which she plopped down not far from the computer.

He noticed her fingers around the edges of them. Remembered how they'd felt on his body.

"It tells us that they don't know you're with me," he said. "That box was left sometime last night or early this morning. You'd already left. Whoever delivered it didn't know that."

She looked up at him; some of the worry that had been a constant in her expression since they'd reconnected seemed to ease. From the moment he'd seen her again, her life had been in danger.

But it wouldn't always be.

He wanted to know her then, too. When she wasn't consumed with worry.

"I have to go out for a while," he pretty much blurted

out. And then added, "And my siblings will be by late this afternoon for a meeting on the case." Just the thought of it—facing his siblings with the mother of his child in their home—set him on edge.

"I'll stay up here."

Her solution eased his tension. But only menially. The girls knew how to climb stairs. And technically, Charlize was in Pippa and Kiely's bedroom.

Some of his discomfort must have shown on his face as Charlize stepped closer, lifting a hand to his beard, smoothing it as she'd done that not so long ago night. Touching him much like he'd touched her only an hour before.

"It's okay, Riley," she told him softly, her gaze knowing. Confident.

Reassuring, even.

"I know this is hard for you…"

"I'm fine," he said. "You're the one whose life is in danger…"

"I wasn't talking about the threats," she said. "I just want you to know, I'm not going to ask for anything, or expect more than you can give," she told him. "And your sisters and brother—they're your family. How all of you handle this whole baby thing…it's up to you. I'll accommodate you as much as I possibly can."

Her hand fell to her side. Which was for the best.

He nodded. Told her she could reach him on his cell if she needed anything, then got the hell out of there.

Pal was on guard, and Ashanti was at the office, too. Though Ashanti wasn't licensed to carry a gun, she was every bit as tough as Charlize.

Bailey pulled in just as Riley was backing out of the double car drive that led to the family parking around back. Good. Though he felt confident that whoever was after Charlize didn't know she was staying with him—or even knew him—he still felt better knowing that the house was well occupied.

He needed to do some drive-bys. To reassure himself that the suspects in Charlize's case were all at work as they were supposed to be. And then he was going to see two separate couples, RevitaYou investors who'd been unavailable for in-person meetings until that day. Frustrated that no one was getting anywhere interviewing any of the users, he wanted to talk to the last few himself.

An hour later he was back at the house.

"How's she doing?" he asked Ashanti as soon as he come in from the kitchen.

From behind her desk, Ashanti shook her head, her long braids accentuating the move. "Haven't heard a peep from her," she said. He wanted to go upstairs. To check on her.

And the strength of that desire was what kept him downstairs, going back to the kitchen to get a fruit and vegetable tray ready for the upcoming CI meeting. He'd cut the fruit first thing that morning, before dawn, because of his inability to sleep well with Charlize right down the hall from him. The veggies were already sliced, as well, giving him not enough to occupy himself in the five minutes he had before everyone started to arrive.

Bailey left, Pal following him outside. Just as Riley was coming up with the need to double-check the ammunition he kept in a locked drawer in his nightstand, and, since he was up there to perhaps knock on the guest's door just to let her know he was back, he heard a car door shut.

And then another.

Bracing himself, he kept his back to the kitchen entry, carried the tray into the dining room, grabbed a beer because something had to go the way he wanted, and took his seat at the head of the table.

He was the head of CI. The boss.

And he'd changed those girls' diapers. Gotten Griffin out of more than one scrap. He'd hauled all of their asses to sporting events, school events and to see their friends, too. His parents had put him in charge. Told everyone to do as he said.

For the first time in a while Riley longed for those days. Longed for a time when what he said was law and no one got to question him.

His siblings came in quietly. Took their seats. So subdued you'd think someone had died. Griffin had a beer. The girls—*women*, Charlize had corrected him— had settled on nonalcoholic beverages.

It had never been so hard for him to meet their gazes, but he did so. One at a time. Looking around the table.

And then said, "I met with Ellis and Reva Layne and John and Cassie Winslow this afternoon." Investors from the last batch—Brody's batch. "Both elderly couples met Wes Matthews at a seminar, as Brody did. Both, fearing fraud now, have filed reports with GRPD. And neither couple had anything new to give us. It's the same story we've heard elsewhere. They meet Matthews at a seminar. Used cash transfers. And all sources of contact have since been cut off. I was hoping someone had gotten into some kind of personal conversation with him—maybe learned something they'd think was innocuous, but that we could use—but none of them had any clue where he's gone, or anything about his personal life. His conversations with them had been all about RevitaYou, period. I promised them that I'd find him, regardless."

Everyone was looking at him, nodding. No one said a word. In the midst of their silence, almost as though prompted by it, he had a sudden vision of the ultrasound screen that morning. That tiny moving form. The silence that was broken by the rapid beating of a very small heart...

"Sadie, have you been able to find anything on this scientist?"

His sister shook her head. "I'm still looking, of course, but so far, nothing. I had a full day today, though. The crime lab was overloaded..."

"Did your department happen to get the box that came over a couple of hours ago? Had a confetti popper in it with a warning?" He was taking them into Charlize territory, but he had to ask.

She nodded. "I saw it come and when I saw Iglesias's name on it, I asked to handle it. We ran it for prints, but there was nothing. And there was nothing else identifying, either. The popper was one in a million. You can get them at any box store in the city, and elsewhere, as well. The box was a small package with any identifiers from a previously mailing completely peeled off. I hear it was left on a doorstep."

Her report, while disappointing, didn't surprise him. He was glad to know that she'd handled it.

"Charlize's," he said, guessing she already knew that. He'd told them she was staying with him. Was that why they were all being so quiet? Out of decorum? Because of his houseguest?

He'd assumed it was because they weren't happy with him.

And that made more sense.

No one had eaten a thing. Everyone else was watching his and Sadie's exchange. He had no idea how to get them all back on track, other than to keep moving forward with the meeting.

"Griffin, Kiely, either of you find any connection between Matthews and Capital X? Any former clients of either?"

Both shook their heads. Kiely detailed the channels investigated and gave a rundown of the areas she intended to check next. Griffin said he had a couple of more people to talk to.

He could only think of one more question pertinent to a sibling meeting. "Anyone hear anything from Brody?" Ordinarily, he wouldn't have asked, confident anyone who had would have contacted him immediately.

Silent shakes of the head were his only response.

He looked at the untouched food in the middle of the table.

"Eat up," he instructed. Took a long sip of his beer. Fought the compulsion to leave the table and head straight for his office, closing the door behind him.

It was the only option that felt at all comfortable.

Ashanti came through, grabbed a piece of celery and cucumber slice off the tray, telling them all good-night before heading through the kitchen and out to her car.

Griffin helped himself to the tray.

"Is Tate back in town?" Pippa asked Sadie.

Good. Right. Riley looked toward Sadie along with the rest of them.

"He's supposed to be," she told them, reaching for a carrot stick, turning it back and forth between her fingers.

"You don't know?" Kiely asked. Riley focused on the exchange, caring very much about Sadie's answers. And glad that they were all talking. Like a family again.

He'd like nothing better than to have Tate Greer out of her life, though had no just cause for the feeling. Some might think he was just struggling because one of his baby sisters was getting married and he was having a hard time letting go. He knew it was more than that.

"Yes, I know. He'll be back sometime tonight."

"You have a flight number, right?" Pippa asked again.

Sadie shrugged, and Riley's unease grew. Determined to stay out of it in case his intervention brought back the irritating silences, he left it to Sadie's sisters to get what they all needed out of her. Confident they'd be as good or better at it than he'd be.

"You think he's cheating on you." Vikki stated things more often than she asked. And she spoke with the confidence only a twin could have.

"No!" Sadie looked around the table. "Of course not."

"You sure?" Pippa asked quietly. Directly across the table from Sadie, she leaned forward. "We're here for you, you know that."

Sadie nodded. "I...just have some things to work out," she said, and Riley quickly filed away Sadie's lack of verbal confirmation regarding her assurance that her fiancé wasn't cheating on her.

Torn between wanting to strangle the man for possibly hurting his sister, and cheering for the fact that there appeared to be a small chance that Sadie wouldn't be marrying Tate, he wasn't prepared when that same baby sister looked at him.

"We're here for you, too, Ri. You know that, right?" Sadie asked.

Awkward! The compassion coming in his direction almost unseated him. Probably would have if Vikki hadn't followed her twin's words with, "You told us not to ask, and we aren't, and we're definitely here for you, but you do understand that, as we've just found out we're becoming aunts, we do need some answers... sooner rather than later."

"Especially since the woman who's carrying our niece or nephew is right upstairs," Kiely said, lowering her voice as though Charlize could suddenly hear them.

He doubted she'd allow herself to listen if she had been able to hear. But knew, based on where her room was located, that unless she'd left her room and was deliberately eavesdropping—which he knew she wouldn't do—she couldn't hear a thing.

"I...uh...hang on a second." He went to his office, sweating, knowing he was making a mistake, but went anyway, and came back carrying a manila envelope, which he tossed into the middle of the table.

Griffin picked it up. Opened it. His brow rose, and he passed the contents to Vikki. She pulled them out. The entire string of photos that had been given to him that morning.

The room exploded into sound then.

Squeals and glee were followed by demands to "let me see." Taking his beer bottle with him, Riley vacated.

Shutting himself in his office where he could get some much-needed work done.

Instead, sipping on his beer, he sat there feeling completely inadequate.

The sensation was new to him.

And he wasn't sure what to do with it.

Charlize munched crackers, waiting for Riley's meeting to end before going downstairs to get something to eat. Skipping dinner hadn't ever been much of a problem for her, but apparently, her child wasn't going to be as easygoing about mealtime.

Her schedule was changing already, and from then on she was going to pay attention to proper nutrition all three meals every day. For a second the thought panicked her. Brought reality on like a huge wave gushing over her head. Overwhelming her. But much like playing in the ocean's waves, it brought excitement, too. She'd checked a couple of times to see if the cars out back were clearing out.

Riley had said the meeting should only last about half an hour. It had been that. And then some. With her headphones on, playing some calming music, she was trying to write up reports from the phone meetings she'd had with several clients that afternoon. One of which had been to Laurene, Ronny Simms's girlfriend, another to both of the Thompsons' cell phones, catching them at work, and to James Barber's girlfriend, as well. She'd listened carefully, asked pertinent questions, figured all three of them could be lying to her, but wasn't sure if they'd been lying about violence in their own homes or outside them. There'd been no indication that any of them had more to hide from her than during her previous meetings.

At one point she was certain that James Barber was the man threatening her. Then just as sure it had been Ronny Simms.

She'd also doubted that it was either of them, too.

Finishing off the sleeve of crackers she'd started on the previous morning—the only time she'd actually experienced morning sickness—Charlize was debating whether or not she should just order out for dinner delivery when her phone rang.

Aunt Blythe. She'd yet to tell her about the baby. Both of her aunts were going to spoil the child like crazy; she knew that.

She picked up and asked her aunt how she was doing, and heard all about the day she'd had, about the ladies she and her sister had had lunch with. And how her sister was a little slower getting around and Blythe was glad to be there helping her—all of which eased Charlize's guilt at being the reason Blythe had been forced to leave her own home.

And then Aunt Blythe told her something else. "The main reason I'm calling is… I thought you should tell that Mr. Colton… I took another one of the RevitaYou pills…"

"Aunt Blythe! Why would you…" she interrupted.

"I know," her aunt interrupted right back. "I just… it's hard enough accepting that I was swindled out of the money, but that I was scammed into believing in a worthless product… I just wanted to believe that there really was a way to get some youth back. I'm not ready to be old yet."

"You aren't old! Not by today's standards with longer life spans! There are women twenty years older than you who still live alone and drive themselves to church."

Not all that many who were that independent, but she knew of one, which meant there were others.

"I'm being silly, anyway," Blythe said. "I am what I am and no pills are going to change that. I just want you to know, to tell Mr. Colton, the pill made me quite nauseated. I'm sure it was that this time because I was careful to pay attention to the other things I ate. I flushed the rest of the bottle. The case is still at home, under my bed, and you can feel free to dispose of them."

Alarmed, Charlize asked, "Are you sure you're okay?" Blythe had always been more of a mother to her than the woman who'd given birth to her. She couldn't lose her now. Not when she was going to need a mother to see her through becoming one herself.

"Positive," the older woman said, sounding stronger than Charlize had heard in a while. Maybe being with her sister, being needed, was good for her.

Maybe having a new baby in the family would be good for her, too. Give her more reason to live. More ways to be needed.

Promising to tell Riley about the pills, Charlize didn't mention the threat she'd received at their home that morning, telling Blythe, instead, that she was firmly ensconced in a safe place and doing just fine. It wasn't time to mention the baby. She needed her aunt to stay right where she was and not be worrying any more about Charlize than she was already doing. Instead, she told her aunt that the threat should be over very soon.

And hoped, for all their sakes, that she was right.

Chapter 14

Appreciating the fact that Charlize had remained upstairs until his siblings left, he texted her as soon as he'd heard them go and then confirmed that they'd all left. Telling her that he was pulling dinner out of the freezer, and inviting her to do the same.

The half-hour meeting had extended to over an hour—mostly with them out in the dining room alone, probably waiting to see if he'd return.

Though he warred with himself, he purposely hadn't done so. With CI headquarters also serving as his home, he had to have firmly established boundaries around his personal life.

They all had their own personal spaces.

And he suspected they didn't leave empty trays in the middle of their own dining room tables. But was glad to see that they'd finally eaten. The manila envelope was there, too, its contents neatly back inside.

Of course, Charlize's gaze would land right there as she came downstairs to join him. She didn't say anything, but he saw her gaze linger there. She'd recognize the emblem up in the corner, designating her doctor's office.

"Do you have rules against eating upstairs?" she asked him, reaching into the freezer for a bag of chicken alfredo and some broccoli. Had she not been there, and with the family worried about Brody, the CI group would most likely have had dinner together that night.

"You can take food upstairs if you'd like, but you don't need to go on my account," he told her, a little disappointed to know that she didn't want to eat with him. But greatly relieved, too. His food was already in the microwave or he'd have let her go first.

"I'm going to be heading straight back to my office," he continued, wishing the ten minutes it took to defrost and cook could miraculously pass in five. "I've got a pileup waiting there for me, not only with RevitaYou, but also with a cold case I'm working for another client."

And Riley had a 7 pm phone call that he hoped was going to blow the Shannon Martin case wide open.

"It's not good for you to be cooped up in just one small room," he said, just as Pal came in through her doggy door and into the kitchen, nuzzling Charlize's hand.

"I don't want to impose," she said, not just patting the dog's head, like someone who wasn't familiar with the animal might do, but scratching the side of her throat, and rubbing a hand down her neck.

"Pal's always happy for the company," he said. "And there's a small family room down the hall off the other side of the office," he added. "You can watch TV or find a book to read. Or whatever. Feel free to make yourself at home."

He wanted to make himself at home. All over her. Wondered if, in all her reading-people ability, she'd ascertained as much.

If so, the information didn't seem to bother her. Charlize was comfortable around him.

And he liked it. Wanted them both to be comfortable enough to get more comfortable. As in, without all the clothes hanging on them.

"I'll probably eat down here," she said, leaning back against the counter as she continued to stroke the dog. "I don't like food smells in my bedroom."

He'd never been an eat-in-bed kind of guy—not the food kind of eating, at any rate. Making a meal of her posed some interesting ideas…

"You showed your siblings the ultrasound photos?"

Right. That provided the cold shower he'd needed.

He nodded. Watched the clock on the microwave tick down seconds, with too many still remaining.

"What did they say?"

Shaking his head, he reached for the rare second beer. Uncapped it and took a sip. Sometimes a guy just needed to be allowed to relax for a second. "I don't know," he finally said. "I didn't hang around."

Her reaction made him defensive. It wasn't the lack of words, so much as the assessing look that came over her face, almost as though she'd quit merely looking at him and was studying him instead.

"I have no answers of my own. How can I be expected to answer their questions?"

"I'm certain that I'm not meant to be married, to raise a family." He said what she already knew, sounding like a broken record even to himself. "And yet, here I am, about to be a father."

She nodded again. Offered nothing but that. And her continued attention. As the microwave whirred.

"I can't just walk away from that."

There. The words were said. An admission made. To himself, first and foremost. To himself, more than her. He wasn't going to be able to walk away.

"So what does that mean?" Her question came with three minutes still left on his dinner.

"I guess it means that we have to figure out some kind of co-parenting plan."

The words struck terror within him. But he knew they were right as soon as he said them.

"I'm not envisioning a fifty-fifty split, or two houses as home. But…something that involves more than just my financial contribution. He or she needs to spend time with me. And my siblings."

It wasn't just his right to claim the time, but his responsibility. His ethical and moral duty. Some might not agree. He kind of wished he didn't see it that way. But he did. He was who he was.

Not sure what to expect from Charlize, he watched her face soften. "I'd like that," she said, sealing his fate.

He'd seen a little moving body. Heard a heartbeat. He'd become a father—whether it fit him or not.

* * *

She hadn't intended to leave her room after dinner. Charlize had eaten downstairs, had even wandered around a little bit, because to know her surroundings was healthy—and because she didn't want to go stir-crazy. The "little" family room wasn't all that little. Six kids could have grown up comfortably in that room, watching TV, playing games. And she discovered a door to a finished basement, too, though she only walked down a couple of steps, didn't really explore that level at all. There was a large bathroom with pedestal sink on the first floor. And a locked room off the main office. She avoided the study.

Everywhere she looked, the wood floors were pristine. Area rugs were all solid wool, the best quality, and freshly vacuumed. She'd gone back upstairs feeling less like a prisoner in her own life.

And more curious than ever about every single aspect of Riley Colton's life. It was like, seeing his home without him there peering over her, blocking himself from her, she could sense a bit of the boy and then young man he'd been, growing up in that house. And she wanted to know them both.

Another place she hadn't looked was behind his bedroom door. There were just some things that weren't smart. And she couldn't afford to borrow that kind of trouble.

If it hadn't been for the fact that she'd been so preoccupied with the journey around the dwelling, with imagining Riley Colton in all of his ages, occupying the space, feeling his presence in every room, and imagining her child growing up with visits to this house, she wouldn't have forgotten the thermos of iced water she'd prepared for herself after dinner. She'd brought the container from home so that she could keep drinking water upstairs just the way she liked it. Ice-cold. And hadn't realized she'd left it down on the counter until almost an hour after she'd re-ascended the stairs, stepping quietly so as not to disturb Riley.

She'd heard his voice coming from behind the closed door of his office. Sounding professional, not personal, she'd noted. And then admonished herself for making the observation. What he did with his life was entirely his affair.

As long as it didn't affect her baby—and since the child wasn't even born yet, who Riley was or wasn't friendly with couldn't possibly affect the baby—then it didn't affect her, either. No matter what her heart or body might try to convince her to believe.

It wasn't even eight yet. Chances were he'd still be working. Leaving her shoes off, she tiptoed barefoot down the stairs, only to have him come barreling out of his office on the way to the kitchen and grab hold of her as he barreled into her.

"Charlize!" He sounded surprised. More than surprised. And quickly let go of her.

Had he forgotten she was there? Perhaps her silent approach hadn't been the best one. And where was Pal?

Almost as though she'd sensed, or seen, the activity in the house, the German shepherd came in through the doggy door. Looked at the two of them and plopped down on a corner of the dining room carpet, lying there watching them.

"I just came down to get some water," she half stammered, trying not to notice how great the man looked, how alive and vital, even after a full day's work, coupled with a good bit of emotional turmoil. She didn't want to disappear back upstairs, to be locked away alone in the back bedroom. She wanted to sit with him wherever he was. To touch him.

And absorb some of the energy that had reached out to her so headily the night she'd met him.

"I was heading in the kitchen for something to drink, as well," he told her, walking beside her. She'd noticed him take a bottle of beer into his office with his dinner. Maybe the alcohol was adding a bit of jaunt to his step.

When he reached for an individual-size bottle of apple juice instead, she couldn't help asking, "What's got you in such a great mood?"

Not that she was judging him, but he'd been verging on disgruntled, at best, since they'd become reacquainted.

"I'm about to deliver some very good news to a young man who's been waiting over a decade to receive it," he told her. His beard seemed to grow in inches as he smiled at her.

Cocking her head, she couldn't help smiling back. "Is it something you can share?"

Nodding, he told her about the disappearance of Shannon Martin over a decade before.

"The case has never been closed, but it's been stagnant for the past couple of years," he told her, walking back through to CI's main office. With her thermos in hand, she followed him, as though on some invisible leash. "Her brother hired me to see what I could find out."

A woman missing more than ten years. That couldn't be good. And yet…

Maybe just giving a family closure, solving the case, was enough of a high for Riley Colton.

"I'm guessing you found something," she said, intrigued. And standing way too close to him. The way he looked at her, drawing her in as though she was an intimate part of his moment, kept her there.

He nodded. Told her about a jazz shoe manufacturing company. About the manager he'd spoken to. And the name of a father who'd been abusing his little girl. About Shannon Martin witnessing the abuse in a back, unused room of the dance studio where she worked.

"I recognized the man's name," he told her. "The guy wasn't just abusing his daughter—though that would have been enough to put him away forever as far as I'm concerned. As it turned out, he was part of something much bigger, sharing pictures on the internet, hurting potentially hundreds more people over many years. Shannon's testimony in his trial had helped tip the scale with the jury, and also established a propensity and an ability to commit horrendous crimes."

"I'm guessing he had a lot of power. And money." She could tell where this was heading. The man must have had the key witness killed. It happened more often than anyone wanted to admit.

Which was why so many in neighborhoods all across the country were afraid to come forward, to speak up. People like Laurene and many of the other women she counseled included.

"He did," Riley confirmed with a bit of a nod, taking a sip from his bottle of juice, still vibrating with... satisfaction, she now knew.

"So now the brother will know...will be able to at least have closure..." She thought about some of the things she'd seen and heard, working with the police and court system, as she was working to protect abused children.

"Were you able to find her body?" she guessed. If the family could give her a proper burial…

Still, she felt awful for them. And for young Shannon, who'd only stepped forward to do the right thing.

"I was," he said. "Sort of. I don't know exactly where…" His sentence was cut off by a knock at the front door, which she hadn't seen used in the time she'd been at his house. She'd only been there for the past twenty-four hours or so.

Still…it felt like she was one of them already…

And that was a very, very dangerous road to walk, she was telling herself as Riley told her to hang on and went to answer the door. Noticing the hand on his gun, his quick glance through the peephole, she was surprised to see how quickly he pulled open the door, as though he'd been expecting someone.

He'd said he was about to give some news…

She'd thought he meant by phone.

She turned to go…

"Charlize," he called to her, "I'd like you to meet a client of mine. Avis Martin."

The brother of Shannon Martin?

In his late twenties or so, the man was stunning to look at. The shoulders, barely tamed by the dress shirt, tapering down to a muscled torso the tie couldn't hide. Long legs in dress pants and slip-ons that walked with authority. If she hadn't been standing there with the only man in the world who could possibly eclipse him, Charlize might have wanted a second look.

As it was she opened her mouth to excuse herself, but Riley spoke first.

"Charlize is…a friend of mine…" The words prevented her from taking another step. He'd just claimed her as a friend. To one of his clients.

That was huge to her. Shouldn't be, maybe, but it was.

"Good to meet you." The other man nodded, his hands in his pockets. Maybe his glance lingered for a second, but no more than that. Expression completely serious, and…guarded…he glanced back at Riley.

"You said you had some news."

"I do. And if you don't mind, I'd like Charlize to be present while I tell you."

News to her. The glance Riley sent her was apologetic. Completely. And while she sensed that he really wanted her there for some reason, a professional one, she also got the idea he'd just figured out that she could be of assistance.

She got it, though. She was a counselor and the man was about to have final confirmation of devastating news.

She suggested they move to the family room. And by the blink of Riley's eyes, the way he cocked his head and frowned a bit, she knew he was surprised that she'd suggest such a thing. She was guessing that the family room was usually off-limits to CI customers, but this wasn't going to be all about business. Avis was never going to forget the coming moments and anything they could do to give him a warm second in those memories, they had to do.

Luckily, Riley didn't argue with her, but rather, followed as she led the man into a room that, as far as he'd have known, she'd never been in.

So she'd just given herself away for the snoop she was. He'd told her she could make herself at home. And could kick her out if he didn't like it. For now her thoughts were only on preparing the man as best she could to grieve his older sister's death.

She sat on the couch. Invited him to take a seat. "I'd rather stand," he told her.

Joining Charlize on one of the three couches in the room—albeit on the end opposite of her—Riley suggested that the younger man take a seat. With a nod, Avis Martin perched on the edge of a chair across from them, his elbows on his knees, hands clasped while his thumbs met and did their own nervous dance.

"As I told you, I have some news," Riley started, looking deadly serious now. "But before we go any further, I need to know if you're capable of keeping this to yourself for the rest of your life. And if, no matter what I tell you, you'll agree to do nothing with the knowledge except find peace from the knowing."

"He can't really make an agreement like that, Riley, not without knowing what he's going to have to carry."

"I disagree," Avis said. "I've been without Shannon for more than ten years. I've learned how to love the spirit and soul that she was. If you're afraid I'm going to try to get some kind of revenge, or get justice…" He shook his head. "What good would it do? Except to prolong the anger. I want to move on, Detective. To have a more normal life. As I told you when I called, I'd like to fall in love, have a family someday. But I can't. Not until I know…it's like I'd be asking a woman to take on a broken man with no answers. One who's always wondering, always looking at women on the street, in stores... I just need to know. To put this to rest."

Riley looked at her, brows raised. "What do you think, counselor? Do you think there's a good chance, given what he just said, that he'll be able to keep his word to leave well enough alone?"

The question was odd. And yet, if they were dealing with some kind of cartel, or mafia connection, she got it, too.

"Counselor?" Avis asked. "You an attorney?" He was frowning, now, too, looking between her and Riley.

"I'm a family counselor," she told him. "A clinical social worker. I'm truly not here because of you," she assured him.

"But you know what he's going to tell me."

She did, of course, because she'd figured it out, but shook her head. "He hasn't told me yet, either."

Avis looked at Riley.

And in clear, concise words, without stating any names or places, he told the young man that his sister had been witness to a crime and had agreed to testify to save hundreds of people from potential further harm.

"Hundreds?" Avis's voice broke. His eyes glistened. Charlize surmised that he'd figured out where this was going, too.

"At a minimum," Riley told him. "Her accounting to the police was the missing piece. It came from out of nowhere, a crime they hadn't even been looking at him for, but it was enough to put him away forever."

If Charlize hadn't already thought herself in love with Riley—only to discover the feeling to be a figment of her own fantasyland—she'd have fallen a little in love in those moments, as Riley's intensity helped the young man feel how important his sister's sacrifice would have been. The incredibly selfless choice she'd made.

"He got to her. Killed her before she could testify in court," Avis said aloud what Charlize had known. His tone was deadpan, but she knew it had to cover myriad feelings it would take months, maybe years for Avis to deal with. She also believed he was finally on the way to finding his own happy, healthy life.

Riley's shake of the head startled her, but she was so focused on Avis, she didn't really comprehend it.

"He's on death row for federal charges."

Tears flooded Avis's eyes then. And Charlize's, too, though that usually didn't happen when she was working. "She succeeded," Avis said, his voice taking on a new note. Satisfaction, at the very least, Charlize's professional opinion told her. A step toward closure.

"She testified and put the bastard away," Riley said.

"Do you know what happened to her?"

"I do."

Lips pursed, Avis nodded, his gaze never leaving Riley. "That's what you needed my agreement for," he said. "I'm not going to get to bring her body home to the family plot."

Riley shook his head. "No, you're not."

Avis stared at him, then very slowly nodded again, his Adam's apple moving up and down as he struggled to control obvious emotion. "Do you know where her body is?"

"No and I'm not going to, and neither are you." Riley's tone was menacing.

"Okay. Seriously. You gave me what I needed." He

stood. Held out a shaking hand. "There is no thank-you that will ever express…"

"We aren't done yet," Riley said, still seated on the couch.

Avis dropped back to his chair.

"Your sister isn't dead, Avis."

"She's not?" Charlize and Avis spoke at exactly the same time.

"She's in witness protection." Riley dropped the news with all of the seriousness that famed program deserved.

"What does that mean?"

"Shannon's name isn't Shannon anymore. She isn't living a life anyone can trace. She can't ever look for you, or in any way attempt to contact you. And if you even so much as say a prayer too loud in her direction, you could be putting her life in jeopardy. Because there are still people who aren't on death row. People who will be looking for Shannon. And if for one second they thought you knew something, or were in contact with her…"

The man dropped back in his chair, his head fully supported by the cushion behind him, and laughed out loud. A hearty, full-bodied release.

"She's alive," he said, as though trying on the words, through a huge smile. "I've learned to live my daily life without her," he said, looking to the two of them. "And you have no idea…no idea…" He stood. "It's like…all these years… I'm free…" He laughed again. "My big sister is out there. Alive. Living life. She wasn't raped or tortured or sold. She did the right thing and…" He shook his head, tears spilling from his eyes. "I just can't believe it. I wish my parents had lived to see this day, but then, they probably already know." He turned a full circle. And then faced Riley, who was standing now, too.

"Do you know anything about her? Is she married? Does she have kids?"

Riley shook his head. "I don't know," he said. "The marshals who contacted me because I was getting too close and needed me to back off can't say, and even if they could I wouldn't ask. Just as I need you to keep your word, and never mention this to anyone. Your safety, and Shannon's, depends on you both going on with the lives you have now—separately."

"I understand," Avis said. "I wish there was some way she could know I know…"

"Maybe she does." Charlize stood, too. "People, when they're related, close, they sense things…"

Not everyone believed in spiritual things, but if Avis did, the reminder would serve him well.

They talked for a bit longer and then she walked with the men back toward the front door.

"You know," Avis said, turning just before they reached the door. "Our father used to say, 'Will it matter thirty years from now?' As though if not, we'd realize something wasn't such a big deal, but suddenly I'm thinking…who knows what the future can bring? By the time we're in our eighties, the danger…won't matter so much. Even if it put our lives at stake. So who knows? Maybe someday, when I'm old and gray I'll be approached by an old lady with my sister's shining blue eyes…"

With another handshake, he thanked Riley again, and Charlize watched as the hard-core ex–FBI agent turned professional investigator patted the younger man on the shoulder, telling him to take good care and call him if he ever needed anything.

She watched and smiled, choked up. She was proud of the father of her child. The work he did. Glad that her baby had him for a father.

Chapter 15

On a high—having what in his life was comparable to Christmas morning as a kid—Riley turned from saying good-night to Avis Martin to see Charlize already heading up the stairs.

But…

He'd turned to share the moment with her. To hear her impressions of Avis. To have her tell him that in her professional opinion, the young man really had been set free and could move forward to the life he'd envisioned for himself.

He was feeling good, and wanted to feel good with her.

Like he and Marisol used to do after they'd closed a case that had ended well. It didn't happen that way all that often—where there was an actual happy ending to a criminal investigation.

The woman pregnant with his child was halfway up the stairs. "Thank you," he called up to her.

When she stopped, turned, her hand on the heavy, well-shined, hundred-year-old banister, his insides gave a jump of approval.

"I was glad to be there," she said. "Thank you for including me."

He nodded. Fingers in his pockets. Wishing there was a way to have them all over her body and then be able to extricate himself from the situation after the sex. Before it required more of him than he was going to give. Only a fool jumped into the middle of a bottomless lake when he knew he wasn't a good swimmer.

"And I wanted to tell you…" She came down a step and he took a step forward. "I spoke with my aunt this evening. She said that she took one more of those pills. Just couldn't believe they were bad, that she'd not only been swindled out of her money, but that she'd also been scammed into believing in a worthless product."

She wasn't coming down any farther. Riley stood his ground, too.

"She got sick, Riley. That's what she wanted you to know. She paid attention to what else she did and ate, and she's certain, this time, that the pill made her really nauseated."

All personal thought fled as Riley's natural radar kicked in. "I hope she's decided not to take any more," he said, on fire in a different way—the right way for him as he thought of the older woman taking ill.

His baby's great-aunt. A warm, loving person who'd be made happy by the presence of a child in her home. A woman who'd helped raise the mother of his.

He had to get this Matthews guy. Find the scientist. Stop the vitamin distribution...

"She assured me she flushed the rest of her bottle and told me I could dispose of the case under her bed," Charlize was saying. If people really were getting sick from RevitaYou...he now had two counts of it making people sick: Brody's girlfriend, whose account he wasn't quite sure he'd believed, and now Blythe. Something had to be done.

"Anyway," Charlize said, turning back toward the top of the stairs, "you did a great thing tonight." She gave him a sideways glance.

Their gazes met.

He felt her calling to him. His bed was there, empty and inviting, just yards away. They were alone...

Except for the baby she carried.

He nodded. "Sleep well," he told her and headed into his office to nurse a painful hard-on. He couldn't remember a time he'd needed sex so badly. Or walked away from the woman he wanted when she so obviously still shared his desire.

He couldn't do that to the mother of his child.

Because he'd have her and then still want to walk away. Whether or not he'd have been able to do so was a moot point. A vitamin on the market that was making people sick was *not* moot. Rerouting his adrenaline to a more productive pursuit, Riley picked up his phone. There might not be anyone he could call at the moment—without more evidence the police couldn't do anything in any official capacity. He couldn't seem to will Wes Matthews's capture, or even, in that second, lasso the scientist behind RevitaYou, but he wasn't powerless.

Opening his Twitter app, signed in on the CI account, he typed.

#RevitaYou People got scammed and product is junk. Reports of illness. Throw out any bottles of the stuff and don't sell it.

Copying the message, he opened CI's Facebook page and Instagram account, as well, sharing the same message.

There. It wasn't enough. Not nearly enough. But it was something.

And then, tweets and posts done, he sat there. Alone. The events of the evening washing over him. He'd solved a case. Hadn't even told his team about it, but Charlize knew.

That was different.

Understandable. She was living there. Avis had come to CI headquarters.

But things were changing. Within him. And within his family, too. Maybe this had all started with Sadie's engagement. Was Tate Greer the good guy he seemed on paper? Did Riley have his back up just because the guy was taking his little sister out from under Riley's thumb?

And now with the baby…shaking his head, he put his feet up on his desk, leaned his head back on the chair and opened a game on his phone. Something to occupy an overactive brain that wasn't cooperating with him—going over and over the same things—and coming up with the same answers, too. It was a no-win situation, that kind of brain spend.

The game timed out on him. Staring didn't tend to score well.

With a flip of his thumb, he opened his Facebook app again. Just to check his CI post. And then he'd get to work. Nine o'clock or not, he wasn't tired and there were always internet searches he could do. Sometimes it just took persistence, perseverance and patience...

His feet dropped to the floor and he sat up.

He had received forty-five comments in less than fifteen minutes. From all over the United States. Quickly opening Twitter and Instagram, he saw the same. Even as he watched, responses were pouring in with people saying the vitamins worked. Some even attached before and after pictures to their replies, and looking at those images, he had to agree he could see a difference. Of course, images could be doctored, but that quickly? And to what purpose?

Were there that many people selling the pills that they'd all jump immediately to its defense?

Not likely.

He scrolled farther, and...wait. Replies about the toxic effects of RevitaYou began to appear.

Putting down his phone, he pulled all three apps up on his computer. Opening replies. Checking profiles.

An hour later he had a physical list of more than twenty-five responses from people, profiles he'd verified from individuals representing pretty much all demographics, all saying RevitaYou pills made them sick.

Now he had something. Phone in hand again, he called Iglesias.

Left a message with the detective that they needed to speak.

And went back to work.

* * *

On Friday Charlize awoke knowing she had to get out of the house. Staying at CI headquarters was keeping her and the baby safe. She was grateful for that. Wanted it. Would stay as long as it took to find whoever was threatening her.

But being cooped up in Riley Colton's space with no break…that just wasn't proving healthy. She was letting him consume her. Everywhere she looked there were thoughts of Riley as a younger man, or Riley in his current life, living all alone in the massive house in which he'd grown up.

She smelled his musky scent from the second she woke up in the morning until she fell asleep at night. Listened for his voice. Or his step on the stairs.

She'd heard him come up the night before. She'd still been lying there awake, thinking about Avis, about the investigative work that had brought the man a resolution that freed up his life. And interspersed with all the other thoughts, she'd laid there burning for Riley. Had heard him come upstairs sometime after midnight. Heard his door close. Listened for sheets rustling, though she knew she wouldn't really be able to hear them.

She had no problem imagining, though. All she had to do was remember the hours she'd spent with him in a luxury hotel room…

Yeah, she had to get out. To get her head back into the real world. Even if only for a few minutes.

She wasn't going to be stupid about it, though. Sending a text to Riley while she munched a cracker in her bedroom before heading into the shower, she asked him to schedule a few minutes for her to leave the house.

He'd responded before she'd even swallowed her second bite.

Where do you need to be and when?

She pondered that. Didn't need to be anywhere. And he was a busy man. Saving lives. Hers included.

Nowhere. Just need to get out.

How about picking up some Thai food and bringing it back here for lunch?

They'd talked about getting takeout from a restaurant in their neighborhood that night they'd been together. They both knew of the Thai place. Considered it a favorite. And ordered the same exact thing, too, when they visited on their own. At the time she'd seen it as confirmation that he was the man she'd been waiting for.

She'd forgotten all about that particular conversation. He hadn't. Which made her warm all over again— exactly the kind of thing she was trying to avoid.

Sounds good, she typed. Because she couldn't think of a rational, shareable reason to reject the suggestion. And because... Thai food with Riley sounded wonderful.

In white capri pants and a white-and-black fitted tunic, with black sandals, she met him by the back door at the exact time he'd given her. She hadn't seen either Bailey or Ashanti as she'd walked by the main office, but she'd heard Riley's voice there.

Either on the phone or speaking with one of his employees...

Pal came walking out to the kitchen with him, and nudged Charlize's hand. With the man in another pair of tight jeans and a gray polo shirt giving her immediate thoughts of getting naked, she was glad for the distraction.

July's humidity hit her as Riley opened the door, and even though she was already hot, she welcomed the reminder of the world outside the cocoon she'd immersed herself in. Lifting her long, dark hair off her neck, thinking she might have been better to put it up, she followed Riley's instructions, keeping his body between hers and the yard, as they walked the few feet to his car. She was guessing it was no mistake that the SUV was parked right outside the door, rather than over by the garage where she'd seen it before.

"I'd like you to keep your GPS function off on your phone and all your apps," he said as they buckled in. "We're dealing with a guy who likely has no way to track anything, no fancy technology and database access that would allow him to do much of anything except look up your address in public tax records, if he even knew to do that, but I'd rather not take any chances," he continued. All business.

He hadn't even asked how she felt. How she'd slept.

Or said "good morning," for that matter.

And she had to admit to herself, his professionalism made the outing easier on her. Whether he knew that or not, was keeping them impersonal on purpose or not, she didn't know.

Though she hadn't even been cooped up for twenty-four hours, it felt like it was longer and she was just glad to be outside. Noticed a bird perched on Riley's fence. The way the sun glinted off the glass in the garage door.

If she hadn't been in danger, she'd have asked if they could walk to the restaurant. But then, if she hadn't been in danger, she wouldn't have needed to ask. She'd have just gone. From her own home.

Sad how one criminal could change her life so drastically that in the space of a few days, a quick drive to pick up Thai food felt like a major outing. The guy might think he was scaring her from helping more people, but his threats to her safety just made her more determined than ever to continue helping victims get out from under abusive control.

"I spoke with Iglesias this morning," Riley said as he started the vehicle, put it in gear. "He visited everyone on the current suspect list at work yesterday. They were all there as expected, though that package could have been left before dawn, on the way to work. He spoke to all of them personally, and seemed a bit uneasy about both Barber and Simms. Got the feeling they were both hiding something, though he found no connection between them. No indication that they know each other. He also said that neither of them were pleased he was there, at their places of employment, asking questions."

They were down the driveway, backing into the street, and suddenly she was half wishing she was back upstairs in the large bedroom that seemed less and less like a cell with every yard she got farther away from it.

She was not going to let them scare her into feeling like she couldn't leave Riley's home. No matter how lovely that cell might be. She'd done nothing wrong.

"Sadie told me last night that she checked the box herself, yesterday, when Iglesias brought it in. They got nothing identifiable from either it or its contents."

Frustration warred with fear—and won. For the moment. Damn whomever thought they could take her freedoms from her. Which was exactly what her abusive clients were known to do. They used fear to keep their partners under their complete control, prisoners of love, or what had once seemed like love, anyway.

"I talked to him about RevitaYou, too," Riley continued, his gaze focused on the road and the area around them, constantly surveilling as he circled around different streets on their way to a place that had only been two blocks away. He was going to approach the restaurant from a completely different angle; she understood that. "After you telling me about your aunt being sick, I acted on a hunch and put the RevitaYou hashtag out on CI's social media accounts, warning people not to take it. The response was unexpected and I made a list of accounts and the people behind them who said they'd also gotten sick off it. Iglesias is following up with those people today."

"Everyone who responded got sick?" she asked, horrified all over again.

He shook his head. "A lot of people said they took it with good results."

"So you think there's a good batch and a bad batch?" She glanced his way, and for a brief second he glanced back.

That one second was all it took for her to see that he wasn't as far away from her as he seemed that morning. The warmth and familiarity burning in that gaze touched every nerve in her body.

"Or there's something in it that people react to differently. Quantity could be a factor, as well."

They'd pulled up to the back of the Thai place.

"Unfortunately, there's no back or side entrance," Riley said, parking close to the building. "I'm coming around and we'll keep you in between me and the building. As we near the front, keep your back to the wall and I'll be right ahead of you."

It felt like overkill, but she didn't complain. As much as she hated being held prisoner to someone else's diseased mind, she liked having Riley there, caring about her safety.

Liked it too much…

She heard yelling before they even rounded the corner, a man followed by a woman. She put her back to the wall as Riley peeked around to the front of the building…

Wait…did she recognize one of those voices?

"It's a couple at the convenience mart next door," he told her.

The female voice came again.

"I know that voice," she said, moving forward enough to get a glimpse of the couple just as the man raised a backhand to the woman.

"That's Laur…"

She didn't get the words out before Riley had left his position, was going for the guy. She heard a shot ring out and started to shake. Took another look around the corner of the building in time to see Ronny Simms running off, with Riley in pursuit. She didn't see a gun, but if Ronny Simms had one, he was in violation of a court order.

Riley was gaining on the thug, and then Ronny

climbed a fence like a backyard rat. As she watched, horrified, still not sure if Riley was hurt, she hurried toward Laurene. The woman would need comfort. Reassurance.

"You!" Laurene screamed at her. "I should've known you'd have something to do with that guy rushing us. Why can't you just leave us alone? Ronny doesn't ever shoot his gun, but with that guy coming at him…it was self-defense. You're going to get him in trouble."

"He hit you, Laurene." She could see the reddening and puffiness beneath the woman's left eye. Kept looking for Riley, but didn't see either him or Simms. She didn't hear any more shots, either. "And he's gotten himself in trouble. If he shot someone…"

Pray God he hadn't…

"He's just mad because some cop came to his work yesterday and now they're looking at him for things and he's going to lose his job. And it's all because of you. He was fine before you started coming around."

She didn't like the anger, but she understood. And felt sorrier for the woman than Laurene would probably ever know. "If that was the case, I wouldn't have been assigned to you," she reminded Laurene. "You said you wanted me to help you find a job so you could get away from him, remember?"

She couldn't see Riley. Didn't hear anything. Dialed 911, just as he came around the corner.

"I lost him." Out of breath, he glanced at her phone. "And I already called it in."

Hanging up, she turned to Laurene, but the woman backed away a few steps and then turned and ran.

"Let her go," Riley told her. "We have no reason to stop her."

As much as Charlize hated to do so, she knew Riley was right. Laurene just couldn't see the truth. Or was more afraid at the thought of life without Ronny Simms than she was afraid of him.

"You're okay," she said, looking Riley over. He was barely sweating. Looked…as vital as ever.

He nodded. "He's a lousy shot. He didn't even get anywhere close to me," he said, moving toward the Thai restaurant and pointing to the fresh slug in the cement of one corner. His attempt at humor fell short.

He could have been killed. Or she could have been.

But if that slug matched the one taken from the brick outside her front door, they knew the person threatening her now. Everything could be over soon.

While the thought brought great comfort, it also came with a tinge of sadness. Depending upon how long it took the police to pick up Ronny Simms, she could be back at her place by dinnertime.

Spending the coming night at home.

Alone.

Rather than falling asleep with Riley Colton right down the hall.

She'd known the time would come. Knew it had to come.

And it still made her sad.

Chapter 16

Iglesias came to the scene himself. Assigned an officer to Laurene, took the bullet in as evidence, expecting it to match the one they'd pulled out of the front
of Charlize's town home earlier in the week. And he
told Riley to get Charlize home, to lock up tight and
stay put. Until Ronny Simms was in custody, he was
an unpredictable land mine.

And Laurene's indication to Charlize had been that
Ronny was blaming everything on Charlize.

Charlize said she was fine, but her lips were white
with tension as they climbed back in the car. And when
she reached for her seat belt, he noticed her hand shaking. Simms had taken a shot at him—a stranger—in
complete daylight and with others around. The guy
wasn't thinking straight.

"Why were they in our neighborhood?" Charlize asked as he pulled into his driveway.

He'd been wondering the same thing. With only one logical conclusion. Because of her.

"He's not going to give up," she said.

"Maybe Laurene knows what he's been doing. Maybe he was heading to your place and she was trying to stop him," he offered.

Even her sigh trembled a bit. "I just need this done."

He reached out a hand to smooth the hair away from her face and stopped himself. He couldn't give in to the need to take her in his arms, either. Things were complicated enough as it was.

"Iglesias said he'd call as soon as Simms is in custody and with an APB out on him, it should be within the hour," he told her and got her safely in the house.

As soon as Charlize was back upstairs—saying she had work to do, and that she was going to try once more to get through to Laurene—Riley filled in Ashanti and Bailey on what had happened. Telling them they could take off, work from home. If by chance Simms knew who he was and tracked them home, wild card that he was, he didn't want anyone else around. Didn't want anyone else getting hurt.

For the same reason he sent a text to his siblings, letting them know of the situation, and asking them to stay away until they knew Simms was in custody. He heard back from all five of them within the minute— telling him to watch his back.

And to let them know if he or Charlize needed anything.

He didn't like being a sitting duck, which was how it felt to him as the afternoon wore on with no news.

He didn't know enough about Simms. Didn't think he was tech savvy, but didn't know for sure. And certainly wasn't going to risk their lives on assuming he wasn't. Didn't know if he'd somehow followed on foot as Riley had driven home. He went out and parked his SUV in the garage so Simms couldn't recognize it sitting there.

And hated that any getaway was locked away in a building separate from the house.

He didn't know if Simms had any kind of training that could make him more dangerous. He'd told Charlize that the guy was a lousy shot, but the truth was, he wasn't so sure. Simms had pulled a gun and had gotten a round off, barely missing Riley, while connecting his fist with Laurene's face.

So maybe the shot the other day at Charlize's house had meant to miss. Maybe that one had just been a warning, as well. Or maybe it hadn't been Ronny.

If so, one thing was clear. Ronny had been pushed too far into a corner.

But they had a name now. An identity. Someone to pick up. That much was good. Not much of a relief, though, as they weren't positive yet that Ronny was the original danger, or a new one. And they also now knew the guy was an immediate, potentially life threatening danger.

By five o'clock, Riley was ready to climb his own walls. Iglesias had called to say that they'd confirmed the bullet coming from the same barrel as the one in the brick at Charlize's house. He'd spoken to Laurene again, who swore she had no idea where Ronny was. They had a car posted at her house. Every law-enforcement officer in the city knew the guy was wanted for attempted murder on an ex–FBI agent, as well as threatening the life of a social worker. And more minor charges, too.

But Ronny was more intelligent than anyone had given him credit for. At least when it came to street smarts. Simms seemed to have vanished into air.

Or was holed up someplace to escape capture—which wasn't the worst thing.

As long as he stayed hidden away, he couldn't get to Charlize.

In a state of supreme overcautiousness, he suggested to Charlize that they eat dinner upstairs. Her room, his, the bedroom neither of them were using, which actually had a "tea" table with two chairs, he let her choose. He just didn't want her on the ground floor where a shooter could more easily take her out through a window even if she was a distance from it. Not with a maniac out there thinking that his troubles would be over if she was dead.

It was also possible that Simms, if he had rational moments, knew he was done. And was just avoiding capture because he didn't want to go to jail.

Or Simms's anger could be in control and he might be trying to take out anyone who pissed him off, Charlize being number one. Because, in a mind like his, he'd think she'd started it all. While Riley had never aspired to be a member of a behavioral analysis team, he'd worked with them enough to know some of the thought processes perps went through.

Riley didn't much care what the man thought; he just wanted him caught. And until that happened, he was going to keep his gun loaded and ready and have Charlize and that baby she was carrying as close to him as he could.

In one sense, Charlize made his job easy—agreeing to his requests affably, making an event out of dinner in the "tea room," as she called it, acting as though eating in an unused bedroom was normal. Not a cause for fear.

In another sense, her easy compliance made the job that much more excruciating. Every smile she gave him, every attempt at normalcy, common conversation, all seemed to have one result—increasing his desire for her. It grew the second he walked in the room with a tray laden with vegetable soup, grilled cheese sandwiches and fresh fruit, and saw her bending over the small table, lighting a candle.

She'd pulled the table to the far, inside wall. Had found a cloth to cover it. And while he'd still been suffering from that glance at her so-sweet backside, she came to remove the napkins and silverware from his tray, setting the table.

"You could have had a beer," she said, halfway through the meal, as he raised yet another bottle of apple juice to his lips. She'd opted for ice water from her thermos.

He shook his head. "Not tonight." Not any night when he was on watch over her, or any, life.

His text chime went off, and, grateful for the distraction, he checked his phone immediately. All five of his siblings had checked in a second time.

"It's Iglesias," he told Charlize. "He says still no sign of Simms. He's helping another detective tonight on a case and will be doing some drive-bys," he finished reading. Leaving out the part where Iglesias warned him once again to stay locked up tight.

Since searching every home and privately owned

crevice in the city was illegal without a warrant, there was only so much any of them could do.

His discomfort due to his arousal aside, they made it through dinner fairly unscathed. There'd been a glance or two when their gazes had locked, but one or the other of them had managed to break the spell fairly quickly.

Spell…even his thoughts were feeling the tension, coming up with a ridiculous word like *spell*…

"I thought you'd been shot."

She'd finished her soup. Was sitting opposite him, arms crossed, those deep, dark eyes focused fully on him. He could feel the trance of her. The way she drew him.

It had been that way the night they'd met. Once he'd seen her, every other person in the room had ceased to exist for him. They'd been…boring…white noise… every single one of them. Except her.

He almost had been shot. He couldn't lie to her.

"I'm scared, Riley. I know better than to let fear get control of me. I know. But… I'm scared."

He'd been scared during the encounter with Simms, too. Not because a bullet aimed at him had nearly met its mark. But because if that bullet had hit him, the next one would have landed in her.

She licked her lips, almost as though she knew what the action did to him. How it made it nearly impossible for him to look away. To think of anything but kissing those lips that he knew to be sweet and sassy. Strong and soft. The things those lips could do…

He knew every single one of them. His body knew them.

And wanted to know them again.

"Make love to me," she whispered. He tried to believe he'd only imagined the words, but he'd watched her lips move with them. Enticing him to be led somewhere he knew he really shouldn't be.

"I know it's only for the moment," she told him. "But I'm not asking for any more than that right now."

She hadn't moved. Was still seated at the dinner table they'd shared, her arms crossed, more like she was warding him off than calling him in. He heard the call, anyway. Felt it.

"It's not right," he told her, meaning to be strong. In charge. But he was hardly able to hear himself, his voice was so soft.

"As long as we're consenting adults, it is," she said. Shaking her head, she still held his gaze. "The world isn't a pretty little wonderland, Riley. It's hard and unpredictable and there are no guarantees…"

She understood. She really understood. That turned him on as much as her lips were doing.

"I just want one night that's real," she said then. "One night where I'm fully aware, not living in some kind of fantasyland. One night…being made love to by the authentic you…"

"I was authentic…" He started to assure her and she shook her head.

"I wasn't," she told him. "I grew up in fantasyland, Riley. My grandparents knew the minute they saw each other that they were going to be married—each knew separately. And their love lasted their entire lives. Both of my aunts…and then there was my mother. The youngest daughter. She wanted what everyone else had—wanted it so badly, she tried to see it in every single man she met. And when one after another didn't work out, she turned to drugs and alcohol because they helped her keep the fantasy alive..."

Her eyes glistened. She was so beautiful, sitting there in the candle's glow. Beyond anything he'd ever imagined he'd see.

"I believed in the fantasy," she told him, and he wanted her to stop talking before she got to the part where she'd stopped believing. And why. He knew where the story was going.

Didn't need to hear the end.

"You want a night without the fantasy," he said.

She nodded. "You were authentic, but I didn't see you authentically."

Knowing that he'd blown her fantasy, that he wasn't the man she'd waited her entire life to find, that he'd been a disappointment, should have been a huge turn-off.

But he was still hard and aching with wanting her.

"There's a crazy man out there who wants me dead," she said. "I can't just sit here living in fear. I want to feel good. Alive. I don't want to walk out of this house after they catch him, not knowing what a night in your bed feels like."

There was no way he could deny her. "I'm still the guy who makes love once, in this case, twice, and it's over." He whispered the words because they had to be said. He'd screwed up the last time he'd been with her. The only time he'd been with a woman without first giving her the score.

"I know."

He stood, his erection painful inside his jeans, held out a hand to her, and, blowing out the candle, led her down the hall.

* * *

Charlize memorized every inch of Riley Colton's body. She asked him to undress, to let her watch, and lay up against the pillows on his king-size bed, fully dressed, cataloging every second. Her romanticized notions didn't exist but she was getting just one night of the real thing and she had a feeling it was going to become the fantasy of a lifetime. Something that would be with her for the rest of her life as they raised their child from different homes and within different families.

The more she was with Riley, the more she believed that she'd fallen in love the night they'd met, just as she'd thought. And maybe he had, too, a little bit. But life didn't always work out perfectly.

Sometimes you had to be thankful for what you had.

She was the only woman in the world having Riley's baby. And because of that child, the man would be in her life forever. She wasn't her grandmother or either of her aunts. She wasn't her mother, either. She was her own woman. A strong and independent woman.

Feeling her power, she stared at his chest as he pulled his shirt over his head.

"I want to kiss every inch of that chest," she told him, not the least bit shy. Or ashamed, either. "I've been thinking about it. A lot."

His gaze darkened. There was no smile showing through his beard. Riley Colton was as serious about making love as he was about everything else he did.

When his hands moved down to the button on his jeans, she let her gaze linger on the flatness of his belly. The small line of dark hair that ran downward from his chest, past his belly button, down to the goods he was about to deliver up to her.

There was nothing she could see that was forty-three about the man, other than the slight bit of gray at his temples. A graying that distinguished him from boys who didn't yet have his wealth of experience.

Experience was good.

Very good.

He'd unzipped his jeans and his penis almost sprang out, only half covered by the black boxer briefs he had on under them. He was solid, bigger than she'd remembered, and there'd been nothing small in her memory. She watched his thighs as they appeared, too, noting the delineated muscles as he stepped up and out of the denim. Not even the dark hair covering them hid that structure from her. And when he was naked, taking a step toward her, she had one more request.

"Turn around."

Cocking his head, he gave her a playful frown. Almost as if to say, "really"?

"I want to see all of you. This is real night, remember? I don't just want glimpses, or partial sight."

With a look that told her she was going to get everything she'd bargained for and then some, he slowly turned, showing her the tightest ass she'd ever seen. Memory of that butt alone would turn her on for the rest of her life.

As it was, Charlize was about ready to come just looking at him. Because it was Riley. One touch to a hot spot and she'd be gone. She could feel it. Her body was wet, ready, and when he came forward again, she opened her arms to him. Needing to get her clothes off so that he could do what he clearly needed to do—sink himself inside her so they could both find release.

She'd never been one to be ready quickly. For her,

sex generally meant a need for a lot of foreplay, but not with him.

Reaching for her pants as he lowered himself beside her, she yanked them down, lifting her hips to get them gone as soon as possible.

"Whoa, there," he said, a hand on hers, halting her progress, not by force, but because she didn't know what was wrong.

"You want the real me, then you need to let me do some of this my way," he told her. "I want to enjoy unwrapping you. Lord knows I've been doing it in my head for days…"

He'd been mentally undressing her? Charlize smiled up at him. Not a grin, a full-blown smile. And raised up to plant her lips against his in a kiss that gave him everything.

Her body. Her mind. And her heart.

As much as Riley needed to be inside Charlize, he didn't want to slide into home. He didn't want the lovemaking to end before it absolutely had to. So he held himself back like never before. Distracting from his own need by paying attention to hers. From her toes to her ears, he tasted her. Noticing when she squirmed, when she moaned, when she giggled. And revisited anything that elicited moans. Again and again.

He'd never held anyone as magnificent as she was. Yet, it wasn't about the looks, although she was about as fine as they came. Or the long, dark hair that draped over her protectively when she sat on top. It wasn't the responsiveness, or even the look in her dark eyes— though it was all of those things.

He didn't know what it was; he just knew that he

was experiencing what would forever be the best night of his life.

There was no tension. No misconceptions. No concern about false expectations. There was nothing but the two of them coming together because their need to do so was stronger than any reason either of them could come up with not to.

He lingered over her still flat belly. Kissing softly. Touching gently. He didn't speak of the baby growing inside her. But knowing it was his gave him a sense of male satisfaction that should have embarrassed him and didn't.

When he couldn't hold back any longer, he poised between her legs, lined up and ready to go, and still held back. "I think I'm going to do this more than once tonight," he said.

"You can do it as many times as you like, Riley, just do it now! Please!" With that last word, she raised up her hips and took him, all of him. Drew him in, holding him tightly, caressing him with her body and inner muscles until he couldn't think. Didn't know.

He moved. Pulled out and went in again.

And when, after only the second thrust, she cried out, pulsing around him, he let go, spilling himself inside her.

It was the first time he'd ever had condom-less sex and it was glorious.

Because of the lack of condom, his bleary mind told him.

But he knew better.

The sex was phenomenal because he was having it with Charlize. And was going to do it again.

As soon as he had a second or two to rest.

Pulling her close, he liked how she fit the crook of his arm, her naked body half lying on his, skin to skin. The weight of her head just above his heart was...nice.

The silkiness of her long hair clothed him.

And life was good.

Chapter 17

Shocked awake, Charlize lay still, heart pounding as she struggled to figure out where she was. What had woken her.

The bed, the sheets, the room were unfamiliar. She was alone.

A shadow moved by the bed. *Riley.*

He put a finger to his lips, telling her to be quiet as he slipped into jeans and grabbed his gun.

Memory came flooding back as she watched him hold his gun in front of him as he moved toward the door.

She'd fallen asleep in his arms. In his bed.

Every muscle in her body shook as she slid slowly, quietly, out of bed, pulled on her pants and a dark pullover shirt of Riley's that was folded on a chair, leaving her underwear by his on the floor.

A board on the stairs creaked.

Someone was coming up and she had no idea how far up he was.

There wasn't just one board, or one spot in those stairs that made noise when you walked up them. They were old wood. They talked.

Simms. He'd found them. It had to be him.

Unless, could it possibly be Brody come back in the dark of the night, with information for Riley? Would the man come upstairs?

With her eyes trained on Riley, ready to receive whatever silent message he sent her, she moved toward the wall, her chest tight, breath coming hard.

Should she hide? Under the bed, in the closet, behind the door…all places someone would look and when he found her she'd be trapped.

Was Ronny Simms in Riley's home? He was after her. She knew that. He blamed her for everything that had gone wrong in his life. Laurene had told her so.

Because he had to blame someone besides himself.

What did she know about him? She tried to think, to know how to help. He lost it if he didn't feel in complete control. Took stupid, irrational risks.

He was armed.

One shot could take Riley down.

But Riley was well trained. And moving toward the door. Alone in the home as they'd been, they'd left it open.

Where was Pal?

She had no idea what time it was.

Midnight? Three in the morning? Close to dawn?

The silence seemed too loud. She couldn't tell what was going on. If the intruder was upstairs yet.

Riley had his back to the wall by the door. With his gun in front of him, peering through the doorway.

Could he see who was out there? Was it Simms?

She focused in the gloom, her eyes adjusting to the dark. She wanted to stay close to Riley. Slid a couple of steps along the wall toward him.

He shook his head and she stopped. Trembling so hard she was afraid she was giving them away.

A hand on her stomach, she feared for her baby. Had to keep it safe...

A step sounded in the hall...she could hardly breathe...stared at Riley...and...felt a surge of nausea as he dove out through the doorway.

A crash and thump sounded in the hallway. It must have been the table at the top of the stairs falling, the vase with artificial sunflowers inside it hitting the ground. She heard a thump, followed by a human-sounding deep growl. Bodies wrestled.

She heard fists hitting flesh and started to pray. Felt hopeless. A gun slid into the room, as though thrown or knocked away.

She started toward it, knowing fear as she never had before. Real fear. She heard another thump, grunts, was two feet from the gun when bodies crashed through the doorway, Riley on top. The guy on the bottom reached for the gun, grabbed it...

"Riley!" she screamed, but too late. The intruder had slammed the butt of the gun into Riley's head and he lay slumped on the floor.

"Now you're mine, bitch." Simms's voice wasn't recognizable, filled with anger and evil and violence, but it was his face coming toward her. All she could see was that face. Those eyes shining a beam of hate.

Charlize wanted to fight, knew she had to fight, and wrapped her arms around her stomach instead, as though she could protect her baby from the bullet that was about to go through her. As though the baby could survive without her.

"You're coming with me," the man snarled, grabbing her by the hair. He could have her hair. He could pull every strand out of her head as long as he didn't touch her belly. "You're going to talk to Laurene, tell her that you were wrong. You're going to tell her to stay with me, you got that?" He continued to growl at her as he hauled her toward the door.

She tried not to look at Riley's supine body—all of the vitality gone. Prayed that he wasn't dead. She couldn't cry. Couldn't lose focus. She had to save their baby.

It was all up to her now.

With the gun in one hand, Simms half pulled, half pushed her toward the stairs. Sunflowers lay scattered around the floor, the vase on its side in a corner. She stumbled; it was all she could think of to do to slow their pace. To give herself another second or two before she was forced down into hell. The man had a gun. Could shoot her at any moment. And he was out of his mind. She couldn't afford to piss him off any further.

She stumbled a second time, started to lose her balance and reached out a hand to catch herself, grabbing at the banister. The movement took her sideways, putting a foot of distance between them. He was yanking so hard at the hair he held, tears sprang to her eyes.

And in that instant, Simms went down. Her head yanked once more, she felt hair ripping and Simms was on the floor, with Riley on top of him.

There was blood on Riley's temple. And in his hand a gun—with the tip of the barrel pushing into Ronny Simms's head.

"Call 911," he said, his tone soft, menacing.

Without another thought she ran for her room, grabbed the cell phone she'd put on the charger before dinner that evening.

Saw that it was just past one in the morning.

And when the dispatcher picked up, she gave her information quickly. Clearly. She dialed Iglesias next, from the number he'd had her program into her phone the day Simms had tried to run her down. Told him what had happened, just as concisely. By the time she hung up, she could hear sirens. Ran downstairs to open the door.

That was when she saw Pal lying on her side in the dining room and started to cry.

Dawn was on the horizon by the time Riley had a moment alone with Charlize. He'd spent a couple of hours in the emergency room, being checked out for concussion, though he knew he was fine, and had just nodded when the doctor told him he had a hard head.

He'd only lost consciousness for a second or two, just enough for Simms to have a chance to get to Charlize, and then he'd lain in wait, knowing he was only going to have one chance to save her and the baby she was carrying for them.

By the time he got back to the house, the police crew was just leaving, having taken the samples and pictures they'd needed so that they could release the crime scene.

CI headquarters, his family home, a crime scene.

Pal had met him at the door, groggy, but wagging her tail. He already had an appointment at the vet when they opened that morning, made through the emergency number. The vet on call suspected she'd either been drugged, or hit on the head. There was no sign of a bump or cuts.

It was Pal's initial bark that had woken Riley to begin with.

He was going to have to text his siblings. Phone calls would be better, but he couldn't do five of those at a time.

Charlize, who'd been checked and deemed fine by medics at the scene, had wanted to come with him to the hospital, but he'd known that wasn't a good idea. Iglesias needed her at the house, needed her statement.

She and Riley had had their night together.

And he'd allowed himself to get distracted. He'd known that he had to keep a close watch, and instead, he'd had sex. And done it so powerfully, he'd fallen into a deep sleep right afterward.

Had he been doing his job, he'd have been more alert. He'd have slept, as he always slept when in the middle of a big job, with one ear open. He didn't know how he did, he just did. Always had.

Maybe it came from innumerable late-night details, babysitting four toddlers while his parents attended affluent parties and political functions.

In forty-three years he'd never screwed up on a watch.

And now he had.

His own child could have died because of it. The mother of his child could have died, too.

As everyone finally cleared out of his house, leaving

him and Charlize alone in the main office, his mind was filled with the apologies he owed her.

Filled with his own mistakes. And with affirmation that he was a man meant to give his life to a job he did better than most. His "calling"—a term he pulled up from verbiage he'd heard his sisters use—was to find justice for others. Not to find a life partner.

"I'm glad you're okay," Charlize said, coming closer, but not as close as he'd have liked. He could see in the straight expression on her face that she knew their night was done. The sun was rising on a new day and they would go forth as the people they were destined to be.

Meeting an exceptional woman, even having mind-blowing sex with her, didn't change who and what he was. Just as it couldn't change the age difference between them.

"I knew the hospital trip was a waste," he told her. But he'd gone. Partially because he was forty-three years old, not twenty-three, and figured he should just be sure. And…so he could get away from Charlize's pull over him long enough to get his head on straight.

When he'd seen Simms pulling her by the hair, he'd wanted to murder the man.

And lock Charlize up someplace where he'd know she'd always be safe.

Neither thought was a healthy one.

You didn't get everything you wanted in life just because you wanted it. And just because you wanted it didn't mean you could have it. Or should have it.

Look at Simms with Laurene. Simms's thinking that he had every right to have the woman he wanted had sent him over the edge.

And yet… Riley couldn't tell Charlize to leave. He

stood there with her, saying nothing, until he came up with, "How's your head?"

He'd already asked, half a dozen times, before he'd left for the hospital.

"Fine," she said. "I have a bit of a headache, but I think it's tension more than anything else. I called my doctor, and based on what the medics said, she said there's no reason for me to come in. She told me what to watch for, and to call her if anything changes."

Simms had had a handful of her hair in his hand, but there were no discernable bald patches on her head. Riley had checked.

"You want some coffee?" He sure needed some. Before he contacted his siblings. Which he needed to do before Sadie got to work and ended up with evidence bags from her childhood home.

She shook her head. "I called Laurene," Charlize said. "Iglesias agreed that I should be the one to contact her. There's no way she could afford bail on an attempted murder charge, and maybe I could help her see the truth…"

Glad to have another minute with her, Riley settled his butt on the corner of Bailey's desk. "How'd she take it?"

"She cried, but I think they were tears of relief," she told him, her tone thankful. "She said that they were in the neighborhood yesterday so Ronny could kill me. Ronny was trying to force her to knock on my door, with him out of sight. She was supposed to cry, say she needed my help and then when she had me out there and distracted, he was going to shoot me from across the street. But she wouldn't do it. That's why they were fighting."

Coldness swept through him, unlike any he'd known. "Is she willing to testify?"

"Yes. Iglesias is over there now, getting her statement. She said that after she got away from Ronny yesterday, she called her sister in Phoenix and she's going to move out there. Get a fresh start…"

She wasn't smiling. It wasn't a smiling matter. But he could tell she was relieved.

And he was proud of her.

"Congratulations," he told her. A job well-done.

In another world maybe they'd go out and get a beer together. If it wasn't five in the morning. And she wasn't pregnant.

"Well… I'm going to head out," she said then. "I've already got my stuff together and an officer is waiting outside to take me home."

He stood. Had had no idea someone was waiting on her.

Wanted to tell her he'd take her himself. Wanted to spend the day with her. Just to make sure everyone was okay.

But knew he wasn't being rational.

Everyone was fine.

Including him.

"Take good care," he said, nodding as he met that chocolate-brown gaze that absorbed him every time.

"You, too." She smiled. Turned to go.

"Charlize?"

"Yeah?"

He didn't know…just had said her name because he didn't want it to end that way.

"I'll call you in a few hours," he said.

"I'll pick up."

Yeah. She'd pick up. She always would. It's who she was.

He'd do the same, too.

And wondered, as he headed upstairs to shower and then text his siblings, if answering each other's calls would ever help with picking up the pieces of the life that had never really been put together, but had just shattered, anyway.

Chapter 18

Charlize spent the first half of the morning, after a shower, resting on the couch with the TV on. She dozed a bit, and then fell asleep, waking after an hour feeling refreshed, if not necessarily happier.

She had many reasons to be thankful. To be rejoicing. Her baby was safe and healthy. She was free! And safe. Could resume her life, go where she wanted to go, move about without looking over her shoulder every second.

The fear...it hung around. She'd already called a counselor she trusted, had a brief chat, but knew enough to accept that the fear would be there for a while. Until her psyche worked through the trauma and she could let it go—or at least store it away in the far reaches of unconscious mind.

Putting on a thigh-length black-and-white tweed,

sleeveless dress, she left her hair down and put in her favorite pearl and onyx plumeria earrings after she finished her makeup. The black flats were new and comfortable. She chose her ensemble carefully—with one thought in mind—to feel good about herself.

It was Saturday, but she had a couple of appointments scheduled that morning—meetings with families who were gone at work and school during the week. One was a home check for a potential private adoption—that one she looked forward to. The other was another domestic violence home visit ordered by the court: a new client and an important assignment.

She hoped it would be a less volatile one than Ronny Simms. But she knew, even if it wasn't, she'd do her job and do it well. Just as Riley's job was something he had to do, hers was, too. Helping families find healthier ways of living and getting victims out of abusive situations, completed something inside her.

With her spirits prepped, she was just walking out the door, intending to stop in at her office before the appointments, when her phone rang. Aunt Blythe.

Her aunt had been on her list to call. She could come home.

When Charlize told her so, figuring she'd tell her about the baby when they were together, offering to pick her up later that afternoon, she was surprised to hear her aunt hem and haw rather than eagerly make plans to be ready.

"I don't want to hurt your feelings, love," she said. "But if you don't mind, I'd like to stay with Grace for a while. Maybe kind of a permanent while. We aren't getting any younger and we've had fun these past couple of days. And… I think maybe she needs me to help around here a bit. She can't do it all as easily anymore, but refuses to hire someone to come in…"

And just like that, Charlize found herself suddenly living alone. She'd lived alone before her aunt had retired from teaching and moved in with her. There were good sides to having the place to herself. She wouldn't have to answer to anyone, or explain her whereabouts.

For another six months.

And then she'd be depended upon twenty-four-seven for many years to come. So yeah, being alone was a good thing. A breather before the summer of her life hit.

She'd finished her appointments, was trying to think of what sounded most good to do next—wander around a store's baby department, maybe look at some cribs, or stop for some of the Thai food she'd never gotten the day before and have a sloth-like night on the couch—when her phone rang.

Pushing the car's hands-free system on her steering wheel, she glanced at the dash to see who was calling.

Riley.

Maybe she should have looked *before* answering.

He'd said he'd call.

She'd said she would pick up, and she did.

He asked how her day had gone as though it was any other day and they'd been talking on the phone for years. When, in fact, until that week, they'd never even had each other's numbers.

She gave him a basic rundown, leaving out any personal thoughts, impressions, feelings, and leaving out client confidential information, as well.

He wanted to know if Blythe was home yet.

She told him no. And nothing more.

He asked about her head, whether or not she'd been queasy at all.

Fine. And no.

Every word he spoke was touching her, with warmth, and a spike to her heart, too. She had fallen head over heels in love with him. She had to accept that.

"I don't believe in happily-ever-after," he said, almost as though he was reading her mind—which didn't surprise her. She pulled over, stopping on a side street by a sign marked public parking in front of an apartment complex.

"I know."

"I've seen too much. Been through too much."

"I know."

"Maybe, if we'd met when I was younger..." His voice faded off. She'd have been in high school if they'd met when he was thirty.

"Maybe I've just lived too long to find an ever after," he said, modifying the statement.

Either that or he was just afraid to let himself feel the full intensity of his most intimate emotions. Maybe because he'd seen too much. Been through too much. He knew the risk, how easily it could all be snatched away, more than most.

"I've put a lot of bad people away over the years," he continued, and she really didn't want to listen to any more. She got the point. Wasn't arguing it. "It's been long enough now for some of them that they'll be getting out. With grudges to satisfy."

"It's okay, Riley." She'd go shopping. Look at cribs. If she went home now she'd just get maudlin. "Truly. I understand."

His silence wasn't good, either. She couldn't look

him in the eye. Didn't know how her words were affecting him. She didn't like not knowing.

"And we're good with the co-parenting thing," he said. They hadn't really talked about it all that much. But she'd said she'd accommodate him and his family.

"We'll need to discuss specifics," she told him. "Children need consistency so there will need to be some kind of set schedule, but we've got time to figure that out."

"Okay." He sounded better. Which made her feel a bit better.

"I do think, at least when he or she is old enough to walk and talk, that you should have nights at your house now and then. It needs to be a place that feels like safety and security." She thought about asking him if he wanted to come with her to look at cribs. Maybe find something portable for his house.

"Iglesias contacted the RevitaYou users today who commented on Facebook and Twitter. Three of them reported more than just nausea. There were severe GI problems."

So much for crib shopping. She knew what he was doing: changing the subject because she'd gotten too close, gone further than he could currently wrap his mind around.

"Thank God Aunt Blythe threw hers away." She said the first thing that came to mind that would serve as a response to his statement. And then, catching up, asked, "Are they going to be okay?"

"They aren't sure. The problems are ongoing."

She wasn't thinking about cribs anymore, either.

"So now what? I mean, people like my aunt, they're out there, taking these things…"

"I'm heading down to the news station shortly. I called earlier and they agreed to meet with me, and to interview Iglesias on air." He named the largest station in the city and a well-known newscaster. "We're going to get the word out, locally, at least, that this stuff is making people sick. They're going to give a rundown on the scam and on the disappearance of Wes Matthews, too."

Because Riley got the job done. One way or another.

He'd told her and Aunt Blythe that he was going to find the man. He'd told Brody that he'd find Capital X and make it possible for Brody to return safely home. Just as he'd promised Charlize he'd see that she made it safely home.

And he had.

This man did what he said he was going to do. He didn't quit until he did.

Her baby was very lucky to have him for a father.

"I was thinking…just been thinking about it on and off throughout the day…we could live together…here." He'd given her no warning, no hint even. Just dropped the bomb in her lap.

"Riley…"

"Think about it. Your aunt could come, too. This place is big enough for all of us. We could convert the downstairs bedroom back into a bedroom and I could take that, letting the rest of you have the upstairs to yourself. If that's what you want…

"Or, maybe, your aunt could have that room and you and I and the baby could have the three rooms upstairs. And if…in the future…there's ever a time when you and I want to…have another night…we could easily do that without it being a big deal…"

But it would be a big deal. Every time. And every night when she slept alone, too.

She didn't want to "think about it." Couldn't afford to "think about it." She'd only been at CI headquarters for three nights and she was already missing being there.

Such a crazy thought in itself. She'd never even met the rest of the family. But staying in their house, knowing they were downstairs sitting at the dining room table with Riley, knowing they were going to be aunts and uncle to her baby, she felt like she knew them all.

And, for a brief time, had been a part of them. She'd slept in the same bed some of them had slept in. Had worked at a desk at least one of them had worked at.

Eaten on a tea table that two of them had had in their room growing up.

"Think about it." Riley's voice came again, his tone softer. Getting close to touching her within the depths she'd shut off to him when she'd left his home that morning.

"I don't have to think about it," she said aloud. And then added, "I can't accept crumbs, Riley."

His silence brought tears to her eyes. When she could stand the quiet no more, she told him she had to go and hung up.

The silence hit Riley hard late Saturday afternoon. His siblings had all descended upon him shortly after his text to them and had hovered on and off—taking turns watching him for any signs of feeblemindedness, he was sure—making him feel like an old man. He'd humored them for a few hours, understanding that they were worried, answered all their questions multiple times. When the younger twins insisted on cleaning the debris from upstairs, including washing the sheets Charlize had used, he'd simply raised a hand toward the upper level and let them have at it.

And then he'd gone to work. Putting his mind to Wes Matthews, Capital X and Brody. Tuning out the world, focusing completely, as he looked through all of the things he knew to find the question that would lead him to a clue that would get the job done.

It's what he did, and did well.

And righted his world again, brought back his peace, until he stepped outside his office to find the house empty.

Quiet.

His siblings had all knocked on his closed office door, at various times, to tell him goodbye. All but Griffin, who'd texted to say he was heading out. He vaguely remembered each of them there.

Bailey and Ashanti weren't typically in the office on Saturdays.

Pal, who'd suffered blunt-force trauma to the lower side of her head but was already showing signs of full recovery, was at the vet overnight, just for observation.

He missed all of them. His annoying sisters and brother, his employees, his faithful canine companion.

And he missed Charlize most of all. Which made no sense to him. She'd only been in his life for less than a week. In his home for a few days.

He was going to be a father. To have a child of his own in the world.

As he walked through the quiet in the downstairs rooms, he thought about growing up in that house. About being a kid. For the first thirteen years of his life, he'd been nothing but a kid. Sneaking food into the family room while he watched TV. He'd dropped a bit of chocolate pudding on the couch cushion one time. Had done everything he could think of to clean up the spot, and then, failing that, had flipped the cushion over, hoping to never get discovered. He couldn't remember what had happened to that cushion, or the couch, for that matter, but he remembered the months he'd spent worrying over that spot.

If he'd have been caught, he'd have been grounded. Not allowed to go with his mom and dad to their functions.

Mostly, though, he'd worried over earning his father's disappointment.

A father's opinions were important to kids.

His kid would need to know that Riley supported them. Was proud of them. Valued them.

How did a loner like him accomplish such a thing?

Children needed their fathers' approval.

Charlize said the child would need consistency. That Riley's involvement would need to be on some kind of schedule.

The only schedule he'd kept since he'd started with the FBI had been case by case. As determined *by* the case.

Same with CI. He and his siblings met as determined by the cases they were working. When a life was in danger, you didn't clock out...

Being a father...a guy couldn't change that. He could only determine how good of a parent he was going to be.

A guy couldn't change whether or not he was one...

There'd been no indication that Wes Matthews had

children. None of the interviews over the past week had turned up any conversation with Matthews in which the banker had referred to any family at all. There'd been no listing of a marriage—at least not in Michigan.

Back in his office, he sat at the computer. Called up one of the hundreds of databases to which he had access.

Typed in Wes Matthews's name and stared at the loading signal on his screen.

It was a long shot. Most times that was what it took to solve a case. Clues didn't usually leave notes on the doorstep...

A listing flashed up on the screen. A date. A city in Michigan. And a name—Abigail. Born...he did the quick math...twenty-eight years before. With Matthews listed as the father.

Wes Matthews had a twenty-eight-year-old daughter.

Riley finally had his break. And work to do.

For the rest of that night he was on the internet. Searching. Going from site to site, database to database, mostly finding nothing or very little. But he knew that the woman was out there.

And so he kept looking. Sometime after seven he found a phone number. Dialed. And was sent to voice mail.

Every hour for the next two hours was the same result.

A little after ten he found an email address.

Urgent matter regarding your father, Wes Matthews, he wrote. Please contact the Grand Rapids Police Department, Detective Emmanuel Iglesias, or myself, Riley Colton, Colton Investigations. He signed off with his phone number and CI's address and closed his laptop.

He could check email on his phone.

He was tired. The headache he'd been nursing all day was making itself more of a nuisance, but he wasn't going to take any of the pain pills he'd been given.

He went to find a beer instead.

And landed on his favorite couch in the family room, with the television on. There were ways to combat silence. And loneliness.

Simple, really.

You spent the night downstairs.

Chapter 19

Charlize slept in Sunday morning. Might even have spent the first half of the day lazing in comfy shorts and a T-shirt if she was one who allowed herself to wallow. Relaxing was all good, but not when it was accompanied by a sadness so deep you could get lost in it.

She was a very lucky woman. Alive. Free. Healthy. Pregnant with the start of her new life.

She had a job she loved. A job she was good at.

A home.

Aunts who adored her, and, when she was ready to let them know she was pregnant, would adore her baby, too.

And…she'd met her soul mate. The love of her life. So he wouldn't be living with her, or she with him, but Riley was going to be in her life, in her child's life. That was good, right?

Or did that mean she'd never fall in love with someone else? Never get married?

Was she thinking she was going to spend the rest of her life alone?

And would that be the worst thing that ever happened? Aunt Blythe had been alone much of her life and she was happy.

Realizing that all she was doing was confusing herself, taking on the world when all she really needed to face was the next hour, then the next day and week and month, Charlize dressed in lightweight leggings, a comfy white shirt and flip-flops and went into the office for a while to catch up on the little things that had been put aside during the past week.

And to prepare for the week ahead, the added appointments to make up for those she'd missed. And then she went for a long walk at Heritage Park. Until the families having Sunday fun days together started to depress her. Then she went to sit in the sand on the shores of Lake Michigan and watch the waves. It wasn't even noon yet.

Of course, the beach was overflowing with families, too, that warm, blue Sunday in July. Families and couples everywhere she looked. Still, the air, the white noise of voices, the happy shrills of children, weren't all bad. They were life. And she was part of it.

What part she played was up to her. She knew this stuff. Counseled women every day she went to work. Riley Colton wasn't going to be the man in her life. She had to accept that.

And move on.

In her mind and in her heart.

Or risk forever being the woman alone on the outskirts, watching everyone else living. She had to take control. To make a plan.

She wanted a family. At least two children. And she didn't want to raise them alone. She wanted to be married. To have a partner in good times and in bad.

So maybe her grandparents had been wrong. Maybe there wasn't just one love of your life. Okay, so Aunt Blythe hadn't found anyone else, but as far as Charlize knew, her aunt had never looked, either.

She knew people who'd been widowed who'd found other loves…

One true love wasn't a genetic concept. It was a belief system. So maybe that was it…she just needed to open her mind to other possibilities. Change her beliefs a bit.

Her phone rang while she was trying that concept on. Riley.

The irony wasn't lost on her.

"Hello." She tried to keep all intimate intonation out of her voice. Yet, be friendly. Practicing for the future when she was married to someone else and they were co-parenting with Riley.

"How are you feeling?"

"Fine."

"Did you get some sleep?"

"Yes."

As badly as she needed to know how he was doing, if his head hurt, how his siblings had taken the news of the Simms attack, if Pal was okay, and anything else that had gone at CI since she'd walked out of Headquarters' doors the day before, she didn't ask.

Taking charge of her life was up to her, and she was going to do it.

"I just wanted to let you know that I've got a lead on Matthews," he said next. "We're having a Colton PI meeting later this afternoon to determine our next moves, and I don't have the guy yet, but we're going to get him, Charlize. And when we do, I'm going to do everything in my power to get as much of your aunt's money back as I can."

"Have you heard anything from Brody?" It was about the case. Her aunt was involved. So she allowed the question.

"No. None of us has. I'm hoping that means he's taking care of himself out there. Laying low."

She hoped so, too. Because Brody Higgins was a human being. And her aunt had liked him.

"I...wanted to reassure you that I'm going to get this guy," Riley said, and if she'd been at Colton Investigations with him, still in his life, she'd have smiled.

The man was as big and tough as they came. And he showed a vulnerable side, too, if you knew what to look for. At least he showed it to her. Or she knew what to look for.

He'd mentioned reassuring her about Matthews twice. Telling her, and maybe himself, that was the reason for his call. The first mention, she'd bought the reason. The second had given him away.

He had nothing else to say, but wasn't hanging up. He wanted to talk to her. To be connected. But he refused to allow himself. So he was repeating the one thing he could allow. It had only taken a day or two of living with him for her to figure him out.

"Was there anything else?"

He'd say no. They'd hang up. And she'd be one step closer to getting on with her life.

"That schedule you talked about previously…do you have any examples of how that might look?"

Schedule? It took her a few seconds to figure out what he was referring to. And then she remembered telling him that his involvement in the baby's life would have to be consistent.

"Set days that you'd visit. Or have the baby over." Typical visitation, like she'd been scheduling and overseeing for clients for years.

"When I'm on a case, if a life is on the line, I might not be able to get away."

So what, he was backing up on the baby now, too? She wasn't going to let him get away with that as easily as she'd let him push her out of his life. Her baby deserved more from his or her father than that.

"So we'll reschedule," she said. "Parenting schedules are often fluid when the parents can get along well enough to make that happen. It actually works best for the child that way. You work within the schedule anytime it's possible, so there's consistency, something to count on, and you're flexible when required, because that's life, too." She was all business, fighting for the future emotional health of her child as she fought for all the children in her care.

"You're really all right with that?"

Frowning, she watched as a six- or seven-year-old boy chased down his toddler sister who was running as fast as she could in the sand and shrieking with delight. The children were keeping her grounded. It was Riley who was upsetting her.

"Of course I'm all right with it, Riley, why wouldn't I be?" she asked, taking a breath to give him a real piece of her mind. To call him on trying to find an excuse to get out of...

"You said set schedule," he told her. "That kids need consistency and since you're in the business to know, I was assuming there'd be a little negotiating."

The boy caught the little girl. Picked her up with both of his arms under her pits and hauled her back to their parents. Or whom she was assuming were their parents. As soon as he let her go, she ran off again, giggling, and he chased after her.

A game? Or a chore?

Thinking of Riley as a thirteen-year-old with newborn siblings, and then a fifteen-year-old with newborns *and* two toddlers, she figured the answer would have been *chore*.

And yet, even decades later, he was still tending to those little sisters. To the point that his freezer and refrigerator were filled with their choices. Home-cooked and all...

"You still there?"

She was. But couldn't be. She had to move on. Away from loving him so damned much.

"By consistency, I meant regular visits, Riley," she said. "Twice a week every week, for instance. Whatever days work for you. And if you have to be gone—as many parents do who travel regularly for work—then you miss a week. Make up for it when you're back. Consistency provides the security to be flexible when life happens or jobs get in the way. The child doesn't worry when you have to reschedule because your consistent visits have taught him that you'll be back. That he or she can count on you. As long as you keep in contact, and reschedule rather than just not showing up."

"But if there's an emergency, if I'm fighting a Ronny Simms or at the hospital getting checked out…and can't call right away…"

"Then the consistency you've already established will have your back."

"Okay, good."

If she hadn't already been in love with the man, she'd have fallen hard just then. He was bringing to fatherhood everything he'd brought to everything else to which he'd committed his life. His siblings. His career. And now his child.

But not her.

Never her.

It was a fact she was going to have to learn to live with. And somehow keep her heart from breaking.

"She's not returning phone calls or emails, and isn't answering her door. I say the next step is to visit her at her place of employment in the morning." Griffin frowned as he spoke. The younger man wasn't eating any of the raisin and cranberry snack mix Riley had put out for the late-afternoon meeting at CI.

"She works at Danvers University," Riley told the team. He'd found out a plethora of information on the woman who'd been unfortunate to have Wes Matthews for a father and would have continued to fill in his siblings if Griffin hadn't interrupted him.

"I go right by there on my way to work," Vikki piped in.

They were as persistent as rabid dogs and didn't even know the most incriminating part yet. Riley almost smiled at the team he ran. Every single one of his siblings did him proud. As human beings. And as investigators.

"Iglesias is planning to be there when Abigail Matthews arrives at her job in the morning," he told them. He'd just finished informing them that when uniforms went to her house earlier that afternoon no one had answered the door, when Griffin had interrupted. "Nothing came up in a search for Matthews's marriage records, but it's possible he wasn't married," he continued with his report. "They're checking on the identity of Abigail's mother now."

"She works at Danvers?" Pippa asked. "What does she do there?"

Exactly. Riley looked around the table. "She's a research scientist…"

Everyone burst into conversation at once. Including Griffin. Everyone but Riley, that was.

Kiely was the one who looked to him first. "Wait a minute. The report from seminar attendees stated that the scientist who was there, speaking to them, was male…"

He nodded again.

"So you think he was fake?"

"Or someone this Abigail woman conned into going in her stead, to give her some distance, since Matthews is her father."

"He could be someone who works with her." Pippa looked around the table as she spoke.

"A graduate student, maybe," Griffin agreed.

It was good to see his brother fully on board again. Eagerly on board. As his team talked, making suggestions with the goal of coming up with an investigative plan, Riley listened, letting them do what they did best.

All of them were dressed casually, shorts, T-shirts. All should have been out enjoying a sunny Sunday afternoon.

But he knew every single one of them was exactly where they wanted to be.

And, again, he felt satisfied with the work he'd done. At CI, and, years before, at home with his siblings, too. They'd spent a lot of their growing-up time with him and they'd all turned out fine.

If he didn't have to be relied upon every day, if he could maintain his single, dedicated-to-his-career life, then maybe, just maybe, he could be a good dad...

Pal barked, a ferocious warning with no regard to having just come home from the hospital and before Riley could do more than stand, a frantic banging sounded on the back door. He glanced to see each of his siblings brandishing guns, which they'd removed from their holsters. They stood as one, all five of them having his back, and Riley hurried through the kitchen, his back to the wall, until he could view the security camera newly mounted not far from the door, giving him a view of the back.

He recognized the woman standing there immediately. He'd been staring at various photos of her on and off for most of the afternoon.

"It's Abigail Matthews," he said under his breath to his team. And then, with a frown, looked over his shoulder at them. "She's pushing a baby carriage."

He dropped his gun to his side as he pulled open the door, but knew that at least two of his siblings still had theirs up and pointing. He could see the tips of the barrels in his peripheral vision.

"I'm unarmed," she stammered hurriedly, stepping

in front of the stroller, as though to protect anything inside from any bullets that might fly. The entire CI team lowered their weapons as Vikki, their soldier turned lawyer, stepped forward to half frisk the woman, and take a peek in the stroller behind her. When Vikki nodded, everyone moved back to allow the clearly agitated woman room to pull her stroller inside behind her. She was taller than Riley had first thought, and was tan and had blond-highlighted dark hair. Dressed in shorts and a blouse, with flip-flops, she could have been any one of his sisters' friends.

"I'm sorry to barge in on you all," she said, looking from one to the other of them. Riley, with a wave of his hand, directed his siblings back to the table, pulling up a chair on a corner between him and Vikki for Abigail. The stroller, with a sleeping baby in it, sat beside her.

Riley couldn't help staring at that stroller, at the small body inside it, picturing himself at the helm of one of those things, with one of those little ones inside it. The stroller looked like it could double as a bed and high chair, too, with all of the pads and bars. It resembled very little of what he'd remembered from his sisters' infancy. He started to sweat.

And felt an odd kind of anticipation, as well.

Maybe he should think about getting a car seat. And a stroller. Just to have for his stipulated visitation times. And get them soon so he could learn how to use them by the time the child came.

Abigail glanced at the stroller, too, seeming to draw some kind of courage from it.

"This is Maya," she said, pointing toward the baby. "She's my foster daughter. I'm in the process of adopting her." The words were offered as though they'd somehow explain why she'd failed to answer Riley's attempt to reach her. And then had just suddenly shown up on their doorstep late on a Sunday afternoon.

Riley glanced at Griffin, knowing the adoption attorney's ears would be perking up, and wasn't disappointed when he saw his younger brother studying both the woman and the child with intense professional interest. If he'd had any doubt that Griffin was fully engaged in helping them get Brody home, that doubt had just been allayed.

"I received your emails and messages," Abigail said, looking at Riley. He didn't bother to introduce the rest of his team. Either she knew who they were or she didn't. Names weren't important at the moment.

"And I got scared," she told them, looking around the table now. "I did some research on you all and figured I could trust you..."

No one nodded, but no one looked away, either. "I have no idea what you know about my father, or why you're contacting me, but..."

"He's missing," Vikki said.

When Abigail nodded, Griffin leaned forward as though ready to leap from the opposite end of the table at any moment. "I tried to call him," she said, shaking her head. "The number I had for him isn't working," she said.

"That's what everyone else is saying," Riley said, studying the young woman, sure he didn't trust her, but not sure how much that mistrust came from who she was, or because of some vibe she was giving off.

"When was the last time you spoke with him?" he asked, to test her as much as anything else.

Shaking her head of long hair, she turned her hazel

eyes on him, meeting his gaze head-on. "It's…been a while. A long while. We're…estranged." She said the word as though it only minimally described her relationship with her seedy father.

"But that's not why I'm here," she said, looking around the table again, and then back to Riley. "After you left that message this morning, I looked you up and saw your social media posts about RevitaYou. I recognized it because a librarian at the university had told me about it. She'd bought some from a friend and after she'd taken it for a couple of weeks, was asking everyone if they could see a difference in her looks."

"Did she get sick?" Pippa asked, her voice filled with urgency.

"No, luckily not," Abigail answered immediately. "I called her as soon as I saw the post, and went over and got her entire supply," she said. "And then I took what she gave me to the lab."

She looked around the table again, and Riley couldn't tell if she was looking more worried, because she was trying to sell them a bill of goods, or because she was truly afraid.

"I broke down the compounds," she said. "And I found something terrible."

"What?" Sadie's tone was sharper than usual.

"There's a compound of Ricin in it that can be deadly depending on the person taking it. Certain bodies will react more strongly to it than others, and it won't affect everyone, but unless this stuff is off the streets immediately, it's only a matter of time before deaths are reported."

The collective gasp that hit the air seemed to strike

the baby, as well. Her feet jerked up, she sucked in air and then settled back to sleep without opening her eyes.

"RevitaYou is deadly," Abigail told them then. "I saw a replay of the newscast that was done last night," she said. "They're saying not only that people are getting sick but also that the banker running the RevitaYou pyramid is my father. Is that right?"

She clearly knew the answer to her question before she'd asked it. Riley could read that much in her expression. And didn't bother answering. He just stared at her. As did the rest of the team.

"And you all think I'm involved," she told him. "I was afraid…as soon as I heard the news…tested the pills… I knew…" She hung her head before Riley could be certain it was tears he'd seen as the sudden sheen in her eyes. And when she glanced back up, her gaze was filled with nothing but fear. Sincere or otherwise.

"I swear to you all. I haven't seen or spoken to my father in forever. You're welcome to my phone records, to anything… I'm working on a memory-boosting drug… something that will really help improve the quality of life, not just improve the appearance of it… You're welcome to check out my lab, my records, anything. That's why I came to you tonight. It's only a matter of time before the police take me in, and I can't take a chance on them taking their time to clear me. I could lose Maya…"

The tears that came to her eyes then were unmistakable.

And Riley glanced at his team. As each one gave a small nod, he told Abigail that they'd see what they could do.

He didn't trust her. Doubted that any of his siblings did. But if what she said was true…

Their mission was to find justice for all they could.

And to bring Brody home.

Not to judge a person by her father.

As they saw Abigail safely out, with Riley's promise to call Emmanuel Iglesias at GRPD and fill him in, Riley hoped that karma had taken note of the choice they'd just made. Because, in the future, he'd hate for his kid to be judged by some of the choices Riley had made.

Chapter 20

Charlize drove to Lowell to have Sunday dinner with her aunts and uncle Sunday afternoon. And while her uncle snoozed in front of a golf match on the television, she led her aunts out to the wicker furniture on Aunt Grace's screened-in porch, perched herself on the daybed she'd jumped on and napped on as a kid, and told them about the baby.

She didn't tell them who the father was. Only that he was a good man who was going to take responsibility for the child, but who didn't want to get married. And braced herself for their questions. Their disappointment.

She was moving on. Starting her new life.

And she couldn't do it without them.

"Oh, sweetie, are you okay?" Aunt Blythe asked,

slowing her rocker to lean forward and gaze into Charlize's eyes.

"I'm fine, Auntie," she said, smiling. "I had the ultrasound this week, and everything's perfect. And I know this isn't the way we wanted it to happen, but I'm really happy about the baby. Super excited, actually…"

"A baby!" Grace said, smiling for a moment. "We're finally going to have a new baby in our family! Just think of it, Blythe." She looked at her sister, frowned at her and then, with a completely serious face, glanced back at Charlize. "What can we do for you?" she asked.

That was it? Was she okay and what could they do for her?

"I know you two have to be really disappointed in me," she said, needing to just get it all out in the open and dealt with so she could move forward.

"Are you kidding?" Blythe stood, came to the daybed, sat down and took Charlize's hand. "You are the brightest shining star in all of our lives, Char," she said. "You always have been. There's nothing you could ever do to disappoint us. It's just not in you…"

"I'm…having a baby without marriage. With a man who's not my one and only. I'm doing just what my mother did…"

The instant and vehement shakes of both women's heads kind of shocked her. "Your mother, God rest her soul, slept with any man who wanted her from the time she was sixteen," Grace said, not with censure so much as with stark truth. "Best as we can figure it was the drugs," she said.

"Or maybe she really wanted what she saw we had, both of us so in love with our husbands, and just didn't want to wait," Blythe added. "She was a spoiled one."

Grace nodded. "Our fault, really," she said. "She was like a toy to us…so pretty and happy to be dressed up. We gave her everything she wanted, even when Mama and Daddy told us not to. We'd sneak it to her…"

"We made her selfish," Blythe said, nodding at Grace.

"That's why she tried to sleep with Harrison," Grace said, referring to Blythe's husband who'd died so young.

"She wanted what I had and didn't think about how it would hurt me," Blythe said.

"Didn't care's more like it," Grace said.

Feeling as though she'd walked into a bizarre twilight zone, Charlize looked from one to the other of them, speechless.

No one had ever, ever told her that her mother was spoiled. And selfish. They'd said it was the drugs. And a desire to find the kind of love they all had.

They'd spun the tale because they were talking to her about her mother.

Looking from one to the other of them, she understood, loved them and felt betrayed at the same time.

When Blythe took her hand, she almost pulled it back, but because of the love, she couldn't.

"We couldn't have you thinking you'd be like her, that you were like her," Blythe said, running her forefinger up and down the back of Charlize's hand. "That's why we didn't tell you some parts of it. The drugs we couldn't hide. You saw the effects of them, but the rest of it…"

She swallowed.

"And after all that, here you are thinking you're like her, anyway…" She broke off. Shook her head.

"So…all of that stuff about love at first sight, about the love of your life…all of that was just part of a fairy tale…" The fantasyland she'd finally given up.

"Oh, no!" Grace stood and came to sit at Charlize's other side. "That part was true. Mama and Daddy fell in love at first sight. I did. And Blythe had her one true love. Just like we told you. And I like to think your mama was looking for real love, too…" She took Charlize's other hand.

"I looked for mine," she said. "I waited…"

"And you found him," Blythe said as though she knew. When she couldn't possibly…

"He's that investigator, Riley Colton," her aunt continued. "I knew the first time I saw the two of you together. The way you looked at him…"

"No." She shook her head as she quickly cut off her aunt, but she didn't let go of either hand holding hers. Instead, she held on tight.

"He's the baby's father, isn't he? This Riley that Blythe's talking about?"

Charlize nodded. "And I do love him…"

"Of course you do…"

Why she'd ever thought these two would doubt her… or had underestimated the support that was there for her…

"He asked me to live with him. Or, rather, to live at his house. To raise the baby there."

"What did you tell him?" Grace's tone had grown serious and noncommittal.

"That I couldn't accept crumbs."

"Thank God," Grace said, while Blythe nodded.

"That's the mistake your mother made," Blythe offered softly. "She settled. And then everyone gets hurt."

"He cares. I know he cares," she said, feeling the despair well up inside her. "But he doesn't believe in love and happily-ever-after."

"Then you made the right choice," Grace told her with enough conviction for the three of them. "A man who enters a relationship he doesn't want or isn't ready for will not be a happy man, and the relationship will suffer. And you aren't a woman who can accept any less than someone being all in."

Having already reached those conclusions on her own, Charlize was still devastated to have them confirmed. Because... "I have no idea who I'm going to live the rest of my life alongside without having him be mine..."

Her voice ended on a wail and slowly, starting one at a time, the sobs came.

Racking, painful, tortured sobs that tore through her, ripped at her throat and expressed the anguish she'd been trying so hard to fight.

Arms around her, Aunt Blythe and Aunt Grace had to have felt every one of them, holding her up, helping her bear them until the tears were spent.

Because they were a family and that was what families did.

The women who'd helped raise her couldn't make this one better. Couldn't put some lidocaine on it, or wash it away with a cool cloth and a cookie. But they'd be there for her.

And somehow, that would be enough.

"Hey, Ri? Can we talk a sec?"

Glancing up from the computer screen on his desk,

Riley saw Sadie standing in the office doorway. He'd thought they'd all left.

"Sure," he said, quickly clicking out of the baby equipment page he'd been just starting to peruse. Kind of relieved to be able to put off what was quickly appearing about to become an overwhelming task. "What's up?"

When she came in and sat in the chair opposite his desk, reminding him of times he'd had to face his father from that very same chair across the very same desk, he wished he had a beer to offer her.

And one for himself, as well.

"I just...you know...with getting married and all... maybe I'm the only one who can see the change in you, and..."

"What change in me?" She was pissing him off and he knew how it felt to sit in that chair and hope to God you weren't about to piss off the man behind the desk.

"This week," Sadie said, looking him in the eye with her chin up, almost as though daring him to argue with her. Almost as though she was the man behind the desk and not vice versa. "You're different, Riley. With Charlize here...it was like you were...happy."

"I'm always happy. I like my life."

"You settle for what you've chosen, yes, and I do believe you're moderately happy with that choice. But this week there was more, Riley, and life should be filled with that *more*. You seem to think that for you it has to be one-dimensional."

He didn't. How could he when he'd never even considered the idea of dimensions.

"It's just that... I hate to think that having all of us come into your lives as we did...you were just a kid and yet with Mom and Dad so busy and preoccupied all the time, we always came to you, depended on you. At least from my memory of growing up it was that way—and now, look at you, living here at home, sitting behind Dad's desk, running the family business… it's like you continue to live that life, to be the one we all rely on, without ever asking anything for yourself."

The fact that she was truly upset had him listening to her, rather than brushing her off, which was what he'd rather have done.

"I'm here because this is where I want to be," he assured her. "I'm good at what I do. Great at it. And it gives me a sense of accomplishment like none other. I had someone tell me once that I'm an adrenaline junkie…"

"Marisol?" Sadie asked. She and her siblings had met his former partner a time or two. He hadn't realized they'd remembered her name. Or anything else about her. It wasn't like he'd ever brought her to family dinner…

"It was obvious you were sleeping with her, Ri," Sadie said drily as he remained silent. "We all knew."

That was news. Not good news.

News better left alone.

"And obvious that you took it hard when she was killed," she added. Delving right into the muck he'd opted to avoid.

Deciding to still opt out, he sat there, saying nothing.

"I just think…it's time that you stop hiding behind all of us, if that's what you're doing, or else thinking that you have to keep sacrificing your own life and wants and needs for all of us, and grab up what you want, Riley. Fight for it, if you have to. Just don't let this one pass you by…"

"Nothing's ever passed me by. Not anything I wanted, anyway."

She shook her head, and he totally recognized the way her eyelids opened a little wider, knowing that she was fighting tears.

"You have to fight for this one, Riley. Fight yourself if you have to. You might not get another chance! For a smart man, you're about the most stupid person I've ever met when it comes to pushing away that which your actions draw toward you."

He didn't relish being called stupid. Most particularly not by his runt of a sister, but she'd made him curious. And pissed, too. Since he wasn't going to spew anger at her, he asked, "What is it that I draw to me?"

"Love," she said. "You make everyone love you to pieces, and then you just push away…"

He stood, angrier than he could remember being at any of his siblings, in a long, long time.

"You think that's what I do?" he asked her, leaning over, his hands on the desk as he brought his face closer to hers.

She didn't rise to meet him. And didn't look away, either. As far as he could tell, she didn't even blink. "I do."

"Well, let me just tell you…" he started, words bubbling up out of deep inside him. "I'm not the one who did the pushing," he said. "I was pushed. Did you ever stop to think about that?"

Frowning, she shook her head. "Could you please sit down? You're towering over me."

He sat. Hard.

Already regretting his outburst.

"What did you mean?" Sadie's voice was soft. Filled with the love that she'd always poured so freely over all of them. "Who pushed you?"

He shook his head. "I was out of line," he said. "I apologize."

"No, Ri, I'm not going away this time. I'm really and truly afraid for you. You really care about this woman. You've got a baby on the way. This is your chance… What did you mean? Who pushed you away? When?"

He wanted to tell her again that he'd spoken out of turn. Spoken nonsense. But as he looked across at her, the little one he'd loved so fiercely and resented at times, too, he opened his mouth, in spite of himself.

"Have any of you ever thought about what my life was like before you were born?" Feeling like he was having a damned pity party, something he abhorred, he reached deep inside himself, knowing the ugly had to come out.

As though he really was in the fight for his life. And if he didn't win, he was going to lose everything that would matter most.

Sadie must have thought his question was rhetorical. Or she just didn't have an answer for him.

He didn't see how answering his sister's questions was going to beat anything, but he said, "I was an only child, Sadie, for the majority of my growing up. I was set in our ways, Mom, Dad and I. We were like the Three Musketeers. When Mom and Dad would go to political functions, or even a lot of times out to social dinners, they'd take me along. I was mature for my age, dressed in a suit and tie, treated like I was a vital part of things. People talked about me following in my father's footsteps. Maybe being governor someday..."

"You wanted to be governor?" Sadie's mouth hung open after she asked the question.

"No." He shook his head. "But I thought I'd be somebody in Dad's world."

"You were. He relied on you constantly when he was prosecuting cases..."

He nodded. Thought about segueing off from where he'd been headed...

"And that doesn't matter, does it?" Sadie asked, her face crumpling as she started to cry. And through her tears she said, quite clearly, "I get it now. I can't believe I didn't see it before." She sniffed. "When they had us, they're the ones who pushed you aside. They didn't take you along anymore because they liked you at home, watching us..." She broke off. Then, with tears welling still, said, "Oh, Ri, I'm so sorry... I feel like an idiot, and..."

"You didn't do anything wrong, Sadie. And I offered to stay home." He told her the truth. He'd offered because he and his mom and dad, out together, it wasn't the same after the twins came. They hadn't been just the three of them anymore. "Mom was going to stay, have me start going places with Dad, and that wouldn't work. I was just a kid. Besides, I thought you all were pretty cool. I got bored at some of those stuffy dinners." True. All true. But it also led to him feeling superfluous in a life he'd taken for granted. In a love he'd taken for granted. Somewhere along the way...was it possible he'd become the giver because he no longer saw himself as the cherished son who'd always be his father's only child? His most prized accomplishment?

The girls had all been so adorable. And two sets of twins… No one had paid attention to the gawky teenager anymore…

"You have to fight for her, Riley. Fight yourself, if that's what it takes. You have to let yourself be loved." Sadie was wiping away tears. He loved her, and all of them, so much.

And he loved his job.

Did he also love Charlize?

"I'll think about it," he told his little sister. There were some things a big brother had to handle on his own. No matter how old and wise the littles got.

"You promise?" she asked.

"Yes."

He'd never broken a promise to any of them. He hadn't made that many of them. Because he didn't make them lightly.

She held his gaze for a long moment and then nodded. But when he'd expected her to stand, to head out, to leave him alone with his twisted-up life, she just sat there.

"Can I tell you something?"

"Of course. Always."

"I'm afraid Tate might really be cheating on me."

All thoughts of his own predicaments fled as he sat forward. "Why?"

"He keeps stepping out to take phone calls, and if I ask who's calling, he brushes me off. Says it's just work. Or something he's not at liberty to discuss…"

"It could be…"

"Yeah."

He didn't think it was.

But wasn't certain that his own prejudice against

the man, for no provable reason, could be clouding his judgment.

"As we've just established, I'm not an expert when it comes to love...but if you're doubting him, you need to trust your instincts. At least listen to the doubts loudly enough to do some further checking..."

"I love him."

"I know."

She nodded. Came around and gave him a hug. Something none of the siblings had done in a long while.

And left him to wrestle with his thoughts.

Chapter 21

Feeling ridiculous for a loss of control that was completely out of character, Charlize drove home Sunday just before six, focusing on the blue skies and sunshine, the vivid greens in the huge trees lining both sides of the road she traveled.

Her aunts had asked her to stay, but she hadn't even been tempted to do so. She loved them. Needed them. But she was ready to have her own life.

To make it the best life it could be. For her baby. And for herself, too.

She spent her days teaching her clients to own their lives, their choices. To believe that they were in charge of their destinies.

To know that the pain of a lost relationship, a lost love, would pass, unveiling a future filled with bright possibilities.

All of the assurances she'd given over the years filled the car, haunting her, as she struggled to apply them to her own life.

So much easier to teach than to do.

And yet…all of the messages she gave to others regarding leaving love behind…the psychological and emotional truths she taught…were based on escaping unhealthy situations—abusive, criminal situations. She also helped families learn how to love each other in a healthy manner.

And sometimes love meant sacrificing herself for someone else.

As long as one didn't lose oneself in the process. And as long as one didn't do all the sacrificing all the time.

As she drove, the setting sun's glare on the bumper in front of her was almost blinding. And then, moments later, around a curve, that same sun gave her crystal-clear vision of the lake she was passing.

The sun. A force they couldn't control. One that blessed them. Lit their way. Warmed them. A trustworthy constant. It might not always be visible, one might not always feel its warmth, but the sun would always be there. It would always rise. It was a force connected to another, stronger than man, source of warmth-love.

And like the sun, just because love couldn't always be seen, or its warmth felt, didn't mean it wasn't there. Sometimes life's clouds got in the way.

Prevented you from seeing clearly.

And then the sun came out again.

Or love showed you the way. A corny line from an old song.

And utter truth.

Riley had lived a long time. He knew what his life had taught him. What his choices had taught him. But he had a huge heart. One that gave and gave and gave.

He'd opened his home to her.

His home, which was a huge part of his heart.

How could she have thought having any piece of that would be mere crumbs?

And how could she hope to have the greatest love of all time by keeping it all to herself? She'd never told him she loved him.

Had never given him her love. She felt her undying bond with him. Knew it to be the once-in-a-lifetime kind. But she'd kept it all locked inside herself.

Love didn't work that way. Couldn't possibly work that way. It only worked when you gave it away.

In her relationship with Riley, he'd been the only one giving.

The realization sickened her. Frightened her.

And pissed her off, too.

She'd been waiting her whole life for one thing, and then, when it finally appears, she screws up?

But what if he rejected her?

How could there be any truly happy future if her once-in-a-lifetime love rejected her?

No. She wasn't going to let the insidiousness of doubt, of fear, prevent her from choosing to try. Choosing to live her best life.

How could she hope to help others make choices that would give them a chance to improve their lives if she couldn't do it herself?

Life didn't come with guarantees. But it came with endless possibilities. With chances. And choices.

Almost home, Charlize made a choice.

A small one.

She turned on the road before the one that led her to her house.

And hoped she was heading home.

Riley wasn't pleased when he heard Pal's bark, followed by a knock at the back door. The dog had been outside and came in, barking a welcome, not a warning.

He wasn't open to any further sibling conversations that night. Not even with Sadie. He needed to work. To spend the evening on the internet, following up on everything Abigail had told them. And looking for things she hadn't said. Connections that could lead them to Matthews.

The woman allegedly hadn't been in touch with her father for some time. She'd said, as he'd asked when she was leaving, that she'd never heard of Capital X and wasn't aware of any of her banker father's associates.

She could have been lying. If he could find anything, a single photo or social media mention, even an announcement of some kind, or an article about Abigail's appointment to her position at the university, anything that could connect someone to both Abigail and her father...he'd have a viable lead.

Instead of finding it, he was dealing with a knock on the door.

His siblings wouldn't knock. They all had keys.

Maybe he'd known who he'd find there the second he'd heard the knock. Maybe he'd hoped she'd be the one.

Maybe he hadn't known or hoped.

Who knew?

Charlize's long, dark hair looked windblown, her

dark eyes wide and imploring as she met his gaze and held on.

"I don't have answers," he blurted in lieu of hello.

She nodded. "I know. May I come in?"

He stepped back. He followed behind her as she made her way through the main office to the darkened family room, turning on lights as she went.

She sat on his favorite couch, the one he'd spent the previous night on. The one with the pillow and blanket still there. She glanced at it, sitting on the end opposite of his unmade bed mess, and, when Pal jumped up, started petting the dog.

Suddenly feeling like one of her clients, like she was there for some kind of home visit, Riley grabbed the blanket and pillow, threw them in the trunk that served as a coffee table and took a seat in a chair.

"I went through a change at thirteen," he said. If she wanted to be a counselor, then she could have it. "I didn't handle it so well, as has been recently pointed out to me."

"Oh? By whom?"

She wanted to know who? Not what?

"Sadie."

She nodded, as though she knew his sisters and the particular one who'd spoken up made sense to her.

"If I had trouble adjusting at thirteen, when I'd be far more flexible and able to cope, how in the hell can anyone think I'd be a success at change at forty-three?"

"Who's asking you to change? Sadie again?"

He stared at her. Needing to be pissed. But struggling to find any strength in the emotion.

"Why are you here?" He asked his own question, rather than answering hers.

"You asked me to give your offer some thought and I have," she said.

His offer?

Growing cold, and then hot, he remembered asking her to live at CI headquarters. She'd said she didn't need to think about it. She couldn't accept crumbs.

"And?"

"I've decided to accept your offer."

He stared. "Did my sister talk to you, too? Is Sadie behind this?" He wouldn't put anything past those sisters of his. They were a strong, determined, capable bunch.

"Of course not," Charlize said, frowning. "I've never met any of your siblings."

Because she'd stayed upstairs when his family had come for CI meetings. And Riley hadn't invited her down to meet them. Purposely. He hadn't wanted the mess.

And yet…it appeared to be sitting in his lap, anyway. Had been ever since Sadie's visit to his office an hour before.

"Are you rescinding the offer?" Charlize wasn't sitting so calmly now. Her chin was tight and a peculiar note of…vulnerability had entered her tone.

She wasn't the only one good at reading people.

"No." He looked her right in the eye. "I think it's the best solution."

"Do you want me to live here?"

"Yes."

"You're sure?"

"Positive." He was.

Positive.

Good to know.

"I want that, too," she said, still sitting over there, so far away. And so…everything…to him. "I just have one condition."

No. She wasn't going to give him this and then take it away. Sadie said he had to fight for himself. For what he needed.

And she'd been right.

So…he'd have to meet the condition. He waited.

"It's not a condition so much as an understanding," she continued, running her tongue over her lower lip as she glanced away from him.

Charlize, unsure of herself?

He was intrigued. And…upset for her, too. But he couldn't fix anything until he knew what she needed. So…he waited some more.

"I need to live honestly," she said. "I need to be able to be myself. Feel what I feel. Share what I feel."

"You sure you didn't talk to Sadie?" he asked, cocking his head. But he was only half-serious. The other half of him was buying time. Whatever seconds he could get.

The rest of his life, of his child's life, of Charlize's life, could be affected by whatever words came out of his mouth next.

Giving him a look that said she wasn't going to be sidetracked, a determined look, Charlize just stared at him.

Time was up.

"I need that, too."

"You do?" Her eyes opened wider.

He nodded. "First up is being honest with myself. I'm not quite there yet, but I'm working on it."

Her smile lit up her small corner of the room. And lit a fire inside him, too.

He wanted her like a son of a gun.

"I'm deeply in love with you, Riley. The once-in-a-lifetime, soul mate, happily-ever-after kind of love. I tried to believe such a thing was just fantasy, but I knew from the first moments I met you that you were the one for me. The one I've been waiting my whole life to find…" She held up a hand as though warding off whatever he'd been about to say. He had no words.

Just a heart pounding so hard he could count the beats.

"But before you go all off on what you can't give, and what you don't want, please understand, I'm not expecting any more from you than you've offered. That's what the honesty is all about. I just can't live here if I have to hide the fact that I'm in love with you. Because, you see, the thing about love is, it comes in all kinds of packages and sizes and shapes, with all different kinds of capabilities. I love you as you are. Who you are. While I believe in love, I also know that life is real. Imperfect. And beautiful with its imperfections. I don't have to have marriage. I just need to be able to give you the love I feel for you. In whatever capacity you can take it."

Pressure welled up inside his chest, cushioning the beat of his heart. Rising to his throat and up behind his eyes.

For a second there he didn't realize what was going on. Didn't recognize the sensation.

And when he did, he quickly froze what was happening to him.

He was not going to cry.

He was going to…

"I love you, too."

Tears pricked behind his lids, and even as he looked at her, his eyes grew a bit moist, but he took them to her anyway, along with the rest of him. Pal, as though sensing the seriousness of her master's situation, jumped down and Riley took her place. Gathering Charlize up into his arms, he kissed her deeply. Showing her things he wasn't sure he understood yet. Things he couldn't put into words.

"I know how to give," he said as, breathless, he finally pulled his lips from hers, leaning his head forward against her. "I know how to have the backs of those I love. How to be loyal. And work hard. I don't know how to let others give back."

But God, he needed to learn. Fast. Because he'd wasted too many years of his life, and there was no way he could deny himself the wealth of experiences Charlize was offering him.

No way he could let himself fail here.

"I'll teach you." Charlize's whisper grazed his lips as her fingers framed his face. "If not with words, then with constancy. Consistency…"

Same as for their child. He almost smiled as he nodded.

But he wasn't done yet.

"If ever there's any threat of danger, you have to promise me that you'll take the baby and go," he said. "That you'll do as law enforcement instructs, no matter what your heart tells you to do…"

"I don't…"

"I need that promise, Charlize. I can't bring you into my life without it."

Her gaze darkened as she studied his, and he knew the second she understood. Even before she nodded.

And then she said, "You do know that there are a slew of FBI agents, law-enforcement officers, and US Marshals who are married, right?"

Of course he knew. And… "A lot of them fail. Because of the job. I can't afford to take that chance." Not when he'd finally found a love all his own.

"Statistically way more lives are lost to car accidents than to violent deaths." She'd apparently come with her own armory full of facts.

"Wealthy people have loved ones kidnapped for ransom," she continued without giving him a chance for response. "So should only those without means fall in love, marry and have families?"

He was getting her point. But pulled away, completely serious. She'd asked to live honestly.

And in doing so, had, in essence, demanded it from him.

"I'm thirteen years older than you," he reminded her. "If we both live to old age, you might end up alone."

"Unless you live to be a hundred and I go at eighty-seven. That would be a pretty good run, wouldn't you say? And with today's longer life spans, entirely possible, too."

He was going to have to hone his debating skills. He could see it now. And he'd thought his sisters had prepared him to hold his own.

"The thing is, Riley, for me, one day is better than none. That's what it comes down to. My bottom line."

One day is better than none. The words were like a bullet upside his head.

"There are no guarantees in life," she said, her tone

soft now, and yet filled with conviction. "But if you open yourself to them, there are endless possibilities."

He was a breaker fully lit. A wave on the ocean, jumping to impossible heights. An adrenaline rush like he'd never known soared through him.

"How do you feel about back-to-back pregnancies?" he asked. "Because if we're going to make that family, we kind of need to get cracking." And he wanted his children to have the comradery that he'd witnessed his siblings sharing their entire lives. A companionship that he'd never known.

He took her grin, her hand cupping his fly, her lips on his, as a positive sign.

And still, as hard as his penis had grown, as much as he ached, he wasn't done yet. Who knew when he'd be able to get that kind of conversation out again. And what he had to say couldn't wait another forty-three years. He pulled his mouth away from hers.

"Charlize Kent, will you marry me?"

The dark clouds in her eyes were a surprise.

"I don't want you asking me just because you think it's what I want or need," she said. "Healthy family relationships have to be based on…"

His lips cut off the professional tone. And he hoped his tongue, his arms, the emotion inside him, would be enough to do the rest.

When he pulled away again, he did so slowly, ready to dive back in again if the rhetoric started spilling again.

"Hi, I'm Riley Colton," he told her. He felt he had to reintroduce himself, since everything had changed between them. A man who most definitely didn't go around asking women to marry him. For any reason.

She grinned, lowered her gaze, almost shyly, and then looked back up at him.

"Charlize Kent, will you marry me?" To his shock, the question wasn't at all hard to ask a second time. He'd repeat it a thousand times if that was what it took.

"Yes!" Throwing her arms around his neck, she pushed him down on the couch, tumbling on top of him, her answer resounding around them.

One word.

One little word.

Out of the billions he'd heard in his lifetime.

And it changed everything.

Riley Colton knew he had finally met his match.

* * * * *

Don't miss the next installation of
Colton 911: Grand Rapids:

Colton 911: Suspect Under Siege *by Jane Godman,*

Available from Harlequin Romantic Suspense
in August 2020!